IRON SNIPER

A World War II Thriller

DAVID HEALEY

D1297373

Intracoastal

IRON SNIPER

By David Healey

Intracoastal Media digital edition published 2018. Print edition published
2018.

This book is a work of fiction. Names, characters, places and incidents are
products of the author's imagination or are used fictitiously. Any
resemblance to actual events or locales or persons, living or dead, is entirely
coincidental.

Cover art by Streetlight Graphics

BISAC Subject Headings:

FIC014000 FICTION/Historical

FIC032000 FICTION/War & Military

ISBN: 0692101241

ISBN: 978-0692101247

CHAPTER ONE

HE WAS a young man in a killing mood. All around him, the landscape was lush and green with summer, but all he saw in the shadowy hedges and copses of trees were sniper hides and the potential for an ambush. That limited worldview had kept him alive so far.

With Micajah Cole, there was always violence simmering just beneath the surface. That violence ran deep as a vein of silver in the Appalachian mountains he called home. Instead of the sun's caress this morning, he felt the cold metal of his rifle and the tension in the trigger beneath his fingertip.

"Will you hurry it up, Hillbilly?" muttered a voice just beyond Cole's right elbow. The voice, with its Brooklyn accent, belonged to Vaccaro. Like Cole, Vaccaro was a sniper, but he was mostly Cole's eyes and ears when he was focused on a target. "The rest of the Army is gonna be in Paris by the time you shoot this son of a bitch."

Cole stayed quiet.

It was mid-summer, 1944. The countryside beyond the Normandy beaches had become a sprawling battlefront more than 60 miles wide, spreading far from the English Channel as Allied troops pushed deeper each day into France. Men and tanks and planes clashed on a vast scale to decide the fate of Europe. Whole towns lay in ruins near the French coast. Thousands had died in the fighting.

None of that mattered just then to Cole. As a sniper, his battlefield had narrowed to 30 feet across the face of a battered stone barn some 200 feet distant. That was the field of view through the telescopic sight mounted on his Model 1903A4 Springfield rifle, manufactured eight months previously at the federal armory on the banks of the Connecticut River in Massachusetts. The Weaver scope—fabricated in El Paso, Texas—had a magnification of 2.5, which meant that the details of the old stone and the cracks of the wood framing sprang much closer. There was no indication of the German sniper within.

In point of fact, Cole's world was even narrower than the field of view of his rifle scope, for of that 30 feet he was interested only in the doorway into the barn. Maybe three feet across and six feet high.

Back home, most barns had big doors for driving a wagon or a tractor through. In his experience, most barns were wooden and even somewhat rickety from storm winds and the lack of repairs during the Great Depression.

Not this French barn, with its stone walls three feet thick. This barn was much older, with medieval dimensions from when a barn door was meant for cows and horses going in and out, rather than mechanized vehicles. A door that size could be closed up tight against wolves, which had still roamed the French countryside when this barn was built. No windows except for two openings in the gable ends. Squat and imposing, the structure before him was part barn and part fortress, really, which was likely why the German sniper Cole was trying to shoot had gravitated toward it.

The gable windows would have been preferable for the

German, but the problem was that the windows faced the wrong direction, looking out across empty fields. It was the barn door that looked out over the dusty road, offering a good vantage point, much like an old 18th-century fort guarding a harbor entrance. From that barn, the German could shoot anything that moved on the road, which had become a problem for the American squad trying to reach its objective.

Vaccaro wasn't one for silence. After a moment he added, "You see him yet? These boys are getting antsy to move on. It's hot out, in case you haven't noticed."

"Then go find yourself some shade, City Boy, and leave me the hell alone," Cole muttered, not taking his eye from the scope.

"Since you asked so nice, maybe I will," Vaccaro whispered, as if the German in the barn might hear them, although that was unlikely at this distance.

It wouldn't be any problem for the German to see them, though.

"Keep your head down," Cole whispered back. The warning was somewhat unnecessary, but it made Cole feel better to say it. Although they had been working together for weeks now as a team, Cole thought that Vaccaro's occasional lapses in horse sense were going to get him killed. Maybe get both of them killed, for that matter.

Cole reckoned he had enough blood on his hands already, so he was making some effort to save Vaccaro's sorry ass. It was a measure of Cole's liking for Vaccaro that prompted him to say anything at all.

"No shit," Vaccaro replied.

Vaccaro fancied himself to be a sniper, too, and he did have a sniper rifle much like Cole's, but that was where the similarities ended. Vaccaro was somewhat better with the rifle than the average soldier, which wasn't saying a whole lot.

Mostly, he scanned for targets using a captured pair of Zeiss-made 10x50 binoculars while Cole stayed behind the rifle scope. Vaccaro also kept his eyes on the surroundings so that Cole could focus on the actual shooting.

If Vaccaro ever felt like second fiddle in the shoot 'em up orchestra, he simply reminded himself that Cole was gifted with a rifle. The hillbilly could shoot the way that Babe Ruth could swing a bat or that Norman Rockwell could wield a paintbrush. They were born to it.

Cole's talent for killing Germans at long range—the Springfield could easily reach out to 600 yards—had not gone unnoticed. Just two weeks before, a famous reporter named Ernie Pyle had written a story about Cole.

"The sniper has a hunter's lean build and clear eyes that must see like an eagle's," Pyle had written in the descriptive prose that brought the war to life for thousands of readers back home. "With a laconic manner and Southern drawl to match, the sniper looks and sounds the part of a mountain man from Appalachia, right down to the Confederate flag painted upon his helmet."

They'd had to ask Lieutenant Mulholland what "laconic" meant.

"If you don't know, then you probably are," he explained. "It's a man of few words."

"That's Cole, all right," Vaccaro said. "Shoot first and talk later."

Vaccaro and the other soldiers had ribbed Cole plenty about the article and about being famous—up to a point. Cole wasn't somebody that you wanted to kid too much. He was laconic, after all.

It was a matter of pride to Vaccaro that Cole had made a point of mentioning him to the reporter, saying that they were a team. It wouldn't do Cole much good to be one of the deadliest snipers in Normandy if some German sneaked up behind him, which was where Vaccaro finally became really valuable. At the moment, however, with an entire squad pinned down behind him, it was highly unlikely that any Germans were going to crawl up Cole's ass.

Vaccaro snorted and muttered something that might have been a commentary on Cole's mother, and then started to reverse crawl back toward a stone wall, behind which sheltered the squad. Silently, they willed Cole to hurry up and shoot the sniper before some officer came along and told them to get moving—right into the line of fire.

For weeks now, American and Allied forces had pushed across France, their objective being to sweep German forces ahead of them. Their ultimate objective was to cross the Rhine and enter Germany, where they could finally put an end to that madman, Adolf Hitler. But the stubborn defense by SS and Wehrmacht troops meant that there was always another field to cross, another barn to capture. Americans had paid for each small victory with blood and lives.

While Cole was well aware of the big picture, none it much concerned him. He was content to leave strategy to the officers. He was focused on that swath of barn that he could see through his rifle scope.

Heat drilled down at midday. While Cole's eyes were focused on the barn, he was aware of the country smells all around him. As a country boy himself, he was reminded of home. He smelled green grass in the sun. Manure. Wet hay moldering where the farmers had abandoned their haystacks to flee the fighting. He registered the stink of a nearby carcass rotting in the heat—maybe a cow, but maybe not.

Cole lay still as a copperhead.

From a strategic viewpoint, the fact that there was just one fairly narrow door into the ancient stone barn had its plusses and minuses. In the plus category was the fact that there was just one approach to defend. In the minus category was the fact that a grenade lobbed through the open door of the barn would turn the German into raw *goetta*, which to the uninitiated was a dish that consisted of loose sausage and mush. Scrapple, Cole would have called it.

At least one brave idiot in the squad had tried that direct approach. Trouble was, not even Dizzy Trout could have hurled a pineapple grenade from the road through that barn door, even though the Detroit Tigers pitcher was leading the American League that summer in strikeouts.

It had been necessary for the soldier to creep much closer, then spring up to throw the grenade. He had been in the process of cocking his arm back for the pitch when the German shot him, causing the grenade to bounce just a few feet away and detonate.

Flies buzzed around the bloody remains. The squad had not sent in a relief pitcher.

Fortunately, Cole and Vaccaro had happened along and were in the process of solving the sniper problem.

Cole thought about where that sniper would be. Deep enough into the barn so that he was hidden in shadow, but not so deep that his own view out would be any more limited than necessary. He would be using something to rest the rifle on, maybe the top of a stall.

Cole did not lack for imagination, but he was equally good at concentration. He had grown up on a hardscrabble mountain homestead where absently walking behind a mule could mean getting kicked in the head, where missing a shot with the one bullet you had in your rifle meant that the family went hungry that night, and where a wandering thought meant that an ax landed the wrong way and took off a foot. A boyhood spent swinging a sharp ax trained one's mind wonderfully in the art of staying focused.

Cole stared into the rectangle of velvety darkness, hoping for some flicker of movement. The sniper, however, did not betray his position. Cole could fire blindly into the barn, but his odds of hitting the German would be slim at best. In the process, he would be giving away his own position for the German to shoot back. He was going to need another plan.

"Hey, City Boy—"

"Goddammit, Hillbilly."

"What? I ain't even asked you for anything yet."

"But I know what you *are* gonna ask."

This was another reason why it helped to work as a team. One man could set up a lure. Snipers relied on subterfuge almost as much as marksmanship.

"Helmet on a stick?" Vaccaro suggested.

"These boys done tried that and he didn't fall for it. Best use Gertrude."

"Poor Gertrude."

Gertrude was the nickname for the mannequin head that Vaccaro had found in what was left of a dress shop. He dug around in his haversack and pulled her out. Made of plaster, with bright yellow hair and lips painted into a red pout, the mannequin head made for such a startling sight as it popped above a wall that more than one German sniper had fallen for the trick, firing at the lure and revealing his position. Gertrude herself had paid a heavy price. There was a bullet-sized divot in her forehead. Most of her right ear had been shot away, so Vaccaro turned the head so that the good ear was toward the barn.

"Get ready, Hillbilly," he whispered. "Here goes."

He lifted the head, keeping his hands below the wall, and almost instantly a shot struck Gertrude. One of her prominent cheekbones vanished in a puff of pulverized plaster. Vaccaro lost his grip on the dummy head, which fell to the dusty road and split in two.

Cole fired at the enemy sniper's muzzle flash.

CHAPTER TWO

IKE LOOKED out at the perfect blue sky of a summer's day and watched a squadron of P-47 Thunderbolts streak toward some unseen target.

"Good luck, boys," he said quietly. "Go get 'em."

The P-47s were more than up to the task, carrying up to 2500 pounds of high explosives in the form of bombs and rockets. Each plane was armed with eight Browning M-2 machine guns, four on each wing, that delivered 800 rounds a minute on targets below. A single plane was almost as destructive as an entire infantry division.

Out the window, the squadron looked no more threatening than a flock of birds in the sky.

It was a hell of a thing, Ike thought, to sit around headquarters, studying maps and looking out the window, not to mention endlessly chain-smoking cigarettes, while young American men fought and died. Ike would not have admitted it out loud, but he also thought with regret of the young German men who were also dying. He saw these German soldiers and the Wehrmacht itself as an adversary, but not really as an enemy—it was Hitler and the rest of his henchmen for whom Ike reserved his real enmity.

General Dwight D. Eisenhower, Supreme Commander of Allied Forces in Europe, was equal parts politician and general. He had to be, because his job involved juggling American leaders and touchy British leaders. The Brits had defeated Napoleon, after all, back in 1812, so they seemed to feel this gave them the expertise to win all over again in Europe. Then there were the Canadians—not terribly demanding, and good soldiers—and the Polish forces, eager for their pound of German flesh. Most difficult of all were the French.

Ah, yes, the French. Some of Ike's colleagues couldn't believe that they had the audacity to want their country back after years of Nazi occupation. The thought made him smile. The trouble was that there were various factions vying for power. They couldn't seem to agree on the future of France.

The Americans and British were backing General Charles de Gaulle, who for all his difficult nature, had a clear vision of a democratic France that aligned with the American and British worldview. Unfortunately, much of the French resistance was controlled by Communists who, on the brink of ousting the Germans, seemed ready to welcome the Soviets with open arms.

The Russians were supposed to be allies, but Ike did not like the thought of liberating Europe from one despot, only to have him replaced by the likes of Stalin.

Ike sighed and stepped away from the window. He turned back to the endless maps and ringing phones.

"Sir, General Patton is on the phone for you. He says he wants to—"

"Tell the general I will call him back."

He didn't have the energy for Patton right now.

Ike lit another cigarette to gather his thoughts. It wasn't quite noon, and he had already smoked a pack. These days, he lived off cigarettes, coffee, and hot dogs. In the evenings, he allowed himself two fingers of bourbon. Sometimes he watched a movie or played cards with Kay Summersby, the pretty young Irish WAC who had started out as his driver and become something more. Nobody was supposed to know that she was his mistress, but it may have been the worst-kept secret at headquarters. Ike was amazed that an entire invasion had been planned in secret, but an affair was impossible to keep quiet. From the strained tone of Mimi Eisenhower's letters, it was clear that the rumors must have reached his wife's ears back home.

The general decided that he would have to deal with that situation when the time came. At the moment, he had a war to win.

The arrival of July put Ike in mind not just of Independence Day, but also of Pickett's Charge at Gettysburg. As a student of military history and of the American Civil War, Ike had stood on that ground at Seminary Ridge and looked across that vast field the Confederates had crossed on July 3, 1863.

In hindsight, the decision by Confederate General Robert E. Lee to attack the Union position seemed like sheer folly. One Browning machine gun could very well have held off Pickett's entire division. Any general who attempted a similar frontal—suicidal—attack today would be swiftly relieved of command, if not sent before a court martial. The Russians seemed to be the only ones who regularly went in for such madness.

Of course, there had been no machine guns at Gettysburg. Ike understood Confederate General Robert E. Lee's vision—or perhaps it was better described as a hope. One desperate gamble, one grand gesture, and the war might be won or lost in a single July afternoon.

Unfortunately, the war in France was not so simple. For starters, there was not one field to cross, but countless ones.

July had come and gone without any version of Pickett's charge. It was now August, and everyone knew that the battle for France was entering its end game.

As a cadet at West Point, Ike had been a pretty good football player. The battle for France was in the last quarter.

On June 6, Allied forces had come ashore on D Day. Operation Overlord had required months of planning and subterfuge to convince the Germans that the attack would come at Calais, rather than at Normandy. While the campaign of misinformation had worked, the success of the landing had not been guaranteed. The weather in early June was stormy, meaning a rough crossing of the English Channel. With only a narrow window of opportunity in the forecast and the tides, Ike had given the order, "OK, let's go."

Those simple words launched the largest amphibious invasion in history.

Thousands of good men had died, although some predictions of the losses had been far more catastrophic. Finally, the Allies had gained a toehold on the beach that June day. From there, day by day, week by week, Allied forces had pushed deeper into Normandy.

But the Wehrmacht was far from defeated. The fighting in the hedgerow country had been particularly savage and favored the defenders.

It was only after Operation Cobra that Allied forces had been able to break free of the awful hedgerow region. Just a few days previously, on July 25, the Army Air Corps and Royal Air Force had dropped millions of pounds of explosives on German positions. Those P-47 Typhoons and the RAF's

Hawker Hurricanes hit German fuel depots, convoys, command posts, troops in the field, and even trains. An unfortunate casualty had been the many French towns and cities in the path of the bombing.

The bombing had done its job, though, by utterly demoralizing German forces and throwing them into a disarray.

With the German stranglehold on Normandy broken, that was when the real charge across France could begin.

"Sir, it's General Patton again. He insists—"

"He insists, does he?" Ike interrupted, unable to hide the annoyance in his voice. "Fine, I'll take it."

He stubbed out his cigarette in an overflowing ashtray, as he girded his mental faculties for a conversation with the general. If it was Tuesday, George Patton would insist it was Wednesday. He was contrary and pushy. He saw himself as a modern-day Alexander, a conquering hero armed with an ivory-handled revolver, rather than a sword. It was only his incompetent superiors who kept him from attaining his full glory. Patton didn't keep his opinion of himself, to himself. He had somehow covered his uniform with more stars than any other Allied general. Ike mused that there might even be more stars on Patton's uniform than could be found in the Milky Way.

For the last year, Ike had kept Patton in the doghouse for slapping shell-shocked soldiers and other general asininity, such as making public speeches that included such nuggets of wisdom as *a soldier who won't fuck, won't fight*. Quote, unquote. Most of the troops loved comments like that; the public back home, not so much.

A hothead such as Patton caused Ike plenty of headaches, but he had his uses. Now, Ike was about to unleash Patton, who was the best battlefield general that the Allies had. The Germans were actually afraid of Patton, which was saying something.

Of course, if Patton had been called upon to navigate a single day of managing Allied headquarters, the war would have been lost by sunset. But for now, Patton and his 3rd Army were just what Ike needed to get the job done of kicking the Germans out of France.

CHAPTER THREE

COLE WORKED the bolt of the Springfield, but held his fire. There wouldn't be any need for a second shot.

He had felt as much as heard the sound of his bullet hitting something wet and solid. Meaty. Like a steak slapped down on a cutting board.

"I reckon that done it," Cole said.

"I hope so, because that was it for Gertrude," Vaccaro replied, looking down sadly at the broken head. "Maybe that's just as well. She was getting heavy to carry around."

They lay there for several minutes, letting the heat soak into them and waiting for any movement from the barn. Cole picked a stem of tall grass and put it in his mouth, sucking at the sweetness. Vaccaro flicked a finger at the pebbles in the road.

But there was only stillness. Then they began to creep forward. When they reached the doorway, Cole nodded at Vaccaro to cover him, and then stepped inside.

He blinked to adjust to the darkness after the bright daylight. He found the sniper's body just about where he thought that it would be. He grabbed hold of the collar and dragged the dead sniper out into the sunlight. It didn't take that much effort. The dead sniper was just a skinny kid. He couldn't have weighed more than a hundred and twenty pounds soaking wet. Blond hair. Staring blue eyes. Did he even understand what he was fighting for? Back home in Gashey's Creek, Cole had a younger brother about the same age. It was a hell of a thing.

"Goddammit," Vaccaro said. "He was just a kid."

Cole stared down at the body without comment.

One of the soldiers in the squad came up and ducked into the barn, emerging with the German's sniper rifle. It was a bolt action Mauser K98 on which was mounted a Zeiss Zielvier 4x scope. All in all, it was a very efficient weapon, produced in large quantities. This particular rifle had been made in Oberndorf. Judging by the dead kid at their feet, the Germans seemed to be running out of actual soldiers, but they didn't seem to have any shortage of weapons. In the hands of a skilled sniper, it had a range even greater than the Springfield. Even in the hands of a half-trained teenage kid, it had been more than deadly.

The GI whistled and held the rifle aloft. "Look at this, fellas. Pretty nice rifle."

"Hey, did he have a Luger on him?" somebody called out. We can't lug around another rifle."

"Give it here," Cole said.

The GI shrugged and handed it over. Expertly, Cole ejected the magazine clip, then pulled the bolt and flung it into the field. Then he took the rifle by the muzzle and swung it against the stone wall of the barn. The scope flew off and shattered, but Cole kept bashing the rifle against the stone, again and again. By then he was breathing heavily.

One of the soldiers started to say something, noticed the look on Cole's face, and clammed up.

Alarmed, Vaccaro spoke up. "C'mon now, Cole. Take it

easy."

Cole kept going until the stock shattered. Only then did he fling what was left of the rifle far into the summer grass. He tossed the broken sight in the opposite direction.

Without a word, he picked up his own rifle and moved down the road.

Vaccaro just shook his head and followed, wondering if his buddy the hillbilly had finally lost it. The thought made him more than a little unnerved. If anyone was born to be a sniper, it was Cole. That hillbilly was a goddamn deadeye. Made you glad he was on *your* side.

If someone like Cole started to lose it, what the hell did that mean for a normal human being?

* * *

THAT NIGHT, Cole wasn't able to sleep. His body was exhausted, but his mind raced. Every time he started to drift off, he saw that dead German's eyes.

He gathered up his blanket roll and his rifle to head outside. The rest of the squad was strewn across the interior of a barn where they had taken shelter for the night, but he had a sudden need to be alone, and to have nothing overhead but the stars and sky.

Through the summer haze, he picked out Scorpius and Lyra and the Big Dipper. His pa, who had known more about the woods and mountains than any man alive, had taught him the constellations—when he'd been sober.

He looked for Orion, the Hunter, but that was a winter constellation.

Looking up at the stars made him feel better. Calmer. People had been gazing up at those same stars since the world began. The stars gave him some perspective on troubles and sorrows.

He had lost his cool today when that dumb cocksucker had grabbed up the German sniper's rifle like a damn trophy. That wasn't like him. Something in him had snapped.

He had needed some time tonight to think it through.

The thing about the Army was, there was never a moment's privacy. From the time you got to boot camp until the day you got your discharge papers, you were constantly surrounded by other soldiers. You ate together, showered together, slept together. Cole supposed that someone, somewhere, might enjoy that feeling of never being alone. Vaccaro came to mind. He thrived on being around other people. Then again, he was a city boy, so what could you expect?

Cole himself missed being alone. He longed for the solitary woods and empty mountain valleys. It was from these empty, lonely places that he gained his energy. Being around people all the time sapped his inner strength.

It wasn't the first time that Cole had gone off on his own. Vaccaro stirred long enough to ask, "You're not worried about some German saboteur coming around to cut your throat?"

"Ain't nobody sneaked up on me yet," Cole said.

He made sure the sentry on duty saw him—no sense in getting shot by your own side—then found a secluded spot and stretched out under the stars.

It was true that Cole was a light sleeper. A boyhood spent hunting alone in the mountains had ingrained that habit. The old-timers called it sleeping with one eye open. Deep in the mountains there were bears, a mountain lion or two, and crazy old moonshiners who would just as soon cut your throat than take a chance that you would rat out their still. Cole would take his chances with German saboteurs any day.

The truth was, he needed some time alone just to think. Cole was no philosopher, but he understood that there was a difference between being alone and being lonely. As much as possible, he put a shell around himself and didn't let many people inside. Vaccaro was an exception. Jolie Molyneaux had been another.

Cole looked up at the sky, guessing that it was close to midnight by the placement of the stars. He never bothered to wear a watch, but could tell time day or night to within a few minutes of the hour.

He realized that something else nagged at his mind. It was like the way that you could tell there was a storm coming. The way the air got very still, and the way that breeze stirred and cupped the pale underbellies of the mountain ash leaves.

You sensed the storm coming, and then you finally heard the thunder.

He wondered if it was Von Stenger.

Was the German dead? That German sniper had shot and badly wounded Jolie, and damn near killed Cole. The experience had left Cole spooked. It was not a feeling that he'd had before, and he didn't much like it. But as far as Cole knew, Von Stenger was dead in a flooded marsh near the town of Bienville.

No, it wasn't Von Stenger. Maybe that particular German would return to haunt him later. This didn't *feel* like him. The storm that was coming for Cole was a different one. But he could sense it all the same.

The coming storm would keep him focused. He would welcome the thunder and rain. He would much rather fight a real enemy than shoot brainwashed kids that had been given rifles.

Lying there under the stars, his thoughts kept flying every which way like they'd been shot out of a scattergun. He needed sleep. Three or four hours of shut-eye before heading back into the field would do him good.

Cole closed his eyes and slept, but deep down, the feral animal part of his mind prowled restlessly, keeping watch, waiting for the storm to break.

CHAPTER FOUR

HIDDEN in the tall summer grass, Dieter Rohde did not look like a stone-cold killer. He was apple-cheeked and baby-faced, making him appear even younger than he was. It was a face that could best be described as boyishly pretty, rather than handsome.

With his helmet off, his dirty blond hair was wavy and too long for a soldier's. Women of all ages often had an irresistible urge to reach out and brush the unruly strands away from his face. They were rewarded with a smile, complete with dimples.

He had the warm brown eyes of a puppy, disguising the fact that he saw with the acuity of a hawk. And Rohde, having been spoiled all his life by women, viewed them in much the same way that a hawk saw a rabbit. Beneath his handsome adolescent appearance lurked a cruel heart.

Peering now with one of those keen eyes through the 4x Zeiss ZF42 telescopic sight on his Mauser K98 rifle, Rohde aligned the single-post reticule on a soldier in the distance. An American.

He had been watching the GI for a while. An entire squad

sheltered in the thick hedgerow behind this one soldier. But this unlucky bastard had been designated as the point man. The scout. If there were Germans guarding this particular field, it was his job to reveal their presence.

To put it another way, the lone *Ami* was sniper bait.

Rohde could easily have taken him, but he bided his time.

Maybe the enemy soldier took some pride in his skills as a scout. He was half hidden behind a stone wall, peering across the field. If he was trying to spot Rohde, he was out of luck. The sniper had hidden deep in the underbrush. He wore a camouflage uniform, which made him stand out from most of the Germans in his unit, but which blended perfectly with the brush. Netting covered his *Stahlhelm*, and he had affixed bits of branches and grass to the helmet to break up his outline even more.

Rohde's rifle rested on a stone. He had put a rag under the wooden forearm to cushion the stock yet more. Anchored by the stone and the French earth itself, Rohde could not have asked for a better rifle rest. Steady as a rock, he could wait all day if need be.

From the brush that disguised him to the sun at his back, it was the perfect sniper's lair. Many of his fellow German snipers working to stop the relentless American advance after Operation Cobra preferred taking up positions in trees so that they had a better vantage point. However, a sniper in a tree could be trapped. It was not convenient to take one shot and move on, which was the best strategy for a sniper who wished to survive another day. Once discovered, a sniper in a tree was nothing more than target practice. The Americans had more than a few marksmen of their own.

Maybe this lone American was one of those marksmen, hoping to set his sights on a German sniper. Rohde kept watch through the scope. Although he handled it with the utmost care, even going so far as removing it at night to secure the optic in a wooden case, moisture had gotten inside and the lens had recently started to cloud over. Consequently, Rohde saw everything now through the scope as if a sea fog was rolling in. But for now, it would have to do. Unless it was the exact same Zeiss optic, affixing a scope to a K98 required the work of a machinist, so it was not a quick battlefield adjustment. Hohenfeldt, his unit's miserly armorer, wasn't about to issue him another telescopic sight, no matter how many *Ami* soldiers he bagged. For whatever reason, fat old Hohenfeldt had taken a dislike to Rohde.

Acrimonious thoughts would not help his shooting, so Rohde put his feud with Hohenfeldt out of mind and focused on what he could see through the slightly foggy scope.

Still, the American lookout had not spotted him. Slowly, the soldier eased over the stone wall and crept into the field.

Rohde let him, keeping watch through the scope.

Next, the American began to cross the field, running in a crouch, his rifle held to one side. Rohde guessed that the weapon was an M1 and he frowned. Like Rohde, most German soldiers were equipped with the bolt action Mauser K98. This was an incredibly accurate and reliable weapon, based on decades of use and refinement since the days of the Kaiser. In fact, the Americans had long ago stolen the bolt action design for use in their own Springfield rifles. Back before the Great War, the Mauser brothers had taken the federal Springfield Armory to court and won a judgment against the armory. It became one of history's ironies that even as the war raged, the United States continued to honor its legal obligations by paying royalties to the Mauser firm.

But in many ways, the Mauser was a weapon from an earlier era, better suited to colonial occupations and the trench fighting of the First World War than to modern warfare.

The rifle had one major shortcoming, which was its reliable and much-copied bolt action design. Each time a soldier fired a shot, he had to manipulate the bolt, which ejected the spent shell. The spring in the magazine then fed a fresh shell into the chamber. Then the bolt was pushed forward, and with a swift downward motion, locked into place. Now the rifle could be fired again. In practice, it took just a second or two to complete this action in the hands of a competent soldier. Unfortunately, working the bolt action often meant that the shooter had to acquire the target all over again.

Given the opportunity for multiple targets, Rohde found this to be a huge disadvantage.

His rifle also had its own quirk in that the bolt tended to stick, forcing him to lock it down using a quick *whack* with the heel of his palm. Again, the motion cost precious time.

The M1 carried by the American was a semiautomatic. This meant that the weapon fired every time that the trigger was pulled. The rifle ejected the spent shell, loaded a new round from the clip of eight bullets, and cocked itself in a *fraction* of a second. The gas operation of the action slightly reduced the recoil. All the while, the shooter could keep his eye on the target. In terms of elapsed time, the advantage of the M1 over the K98 would seem to be an infinitesimal one, but in combat conditions the improved rate of fire was a huge asset.

Rohde wanted one of those semiautomatics. He wished for something new and modern. Not an M1, but the German version known as the Gewehr 43. There were even a few sniper versions outfitted with telescopic sights. They were few and far between in Normandy, but Rohde knew for a fact that that fat sausage of an armorer Hohenfeldt had one such rifle sitting unused, if one could believe it.

Again, Rohde forced himself to focus on the task at hand. Through the scope, he followed the progress of the American across the field.

Now that the soldier was halfway across, the American appeared to relax. He stood straighter. Before, he'd been hunched over. His gait seemed easier. He seemed to be thinking that if he'd made it this far, then nobody was going to shoot at him.

The sun was shining; it was too nice of a summer day to die.

The soldier kept going, and again, Rohde let him.

The sun beat down and turned the exterior of Rohde's helmet as warm as a teapot. Rivulets of sweat ran down his handsome face. Some of that sweat dripped past his eyebrow and into his eyes, the salt stinging. He blinked to clear his vision.

Attracted by the moisture, an ant crawled up Rohde's neck. Its tiny mandibles sank into the sweetness of human flesh, sampling the possibilities it offered. Rohde ignored the stinging. A red welt blossomed on his neck.

Other insects buzzed in the tall grass around him. A bird landed in a nearby bush, oblivious to the motionless human just feet away. Farther off was the chatter of a machine gun, a reminder that instant death lurked on this summer day.

Two hundred feet away, the American was now halfway across the field. Obliviously running at an oblique angle closer to the sniper.

This was as close as Rohde ever been to an American, not counting dead ones.

He heard a sound behind him. Someone heavy crawling through the brush. Trying to be stealthy about it, but making as much noise as an entire squad. He didn't take his eye off the scope because he knew who it was. If it had been an American coming up behind him, Rohde would already be dead.

"What are you waiting for? Shoot him, Rohde."

The disembodied voice belonged to Hauptmann Fischer.

Fischer had displayed a fascination on more than one occasion with snipers, or *Jäger* as they were sometimes known in the Wehrmacht. The German word meant *hunter*. Rohde half expected the impatient captain to take the rifle himself. It was Fischer, after all, who had seen Rohde's talent and put the sniper rifle in his hands. Rohde had become his special prodigy, his secret weapon.

Up close, Fischer had a masculine smell of Sandalwood-scented aftershave mixed with tobacco and fresh sweat. Even now, he managed to be cleanly shaven, his uniform neat except for a few burrs that now clung to it thanks to his crawl toward Rohde's position.

His neat appearance could have seemed prissy or affected in another officer, but Fischer had made it clear to the men in his command that appearance was synonymous with competence.

Rohde liked Fischer, even if he was wary of his increasingly frequent fits of temper. He was a capable officer from a Prussian military family, but like the Mauser rifle, he belonged to an earlier age. The Hauptmann would have been happier walking shoulder to shoulder in organized ranks toward the orderly files of Napoleon's army, for example. Volleys of musket fire could then be exchanged at close quarters, with the engagement settled by a bayonet charge. The officers might seek each other out and fight with swords, like gentlemen.

While the Hauptmann might have preferred a more organized form of battle, he remained a realist. Fischer seemed to find this business of crawling about on one's belly to be distasteful, even undignified, but that was modern warfare for you. He did not find it at all odd when German generals swallowed sodium cyanide—or the muzzles of their own pistols—when they had failed in their duty. It never occurred to a disgraced American or English general to shoot himself; most of them went home and ran for political office. Fischer took this as another indicator of German military superiority.

Fischer was a good soldier, but the long war was wearing him down. Still in his twenties, he was only somewhat older and more worldly than most of the troops he commanded. Lately, the replacement troops tended to be younger and younger to the point that he felt more like their father rather than an older brother. He had been a lieutenant for much of the war, but promotion was coming more quickly these days. At the rate the Wehrmacht was losing its officer corps in battle, he liked to joke that he might be a general by the end of the year.

He was a little too smart for his own good and in the heat of the moment he sometimes made deprecating comments about the German war effort that would have been dangerous if overheard by the wrong people.

Lately, he had developed a very bad temper. He had punched or slapped more than one soldier, and his men were sure that it was only a matter of time before he shot someone as a disciplinary measure. Such things were allowed in the Wehrmacht. In Fischer's case, his anger was a symptom of combat fatigue. But like his men, he had no choice but to go on until the bitter end.

While Fischer was Rohde's champion in granting him sniper status, he had also made it clear that he was still passing judgment on Rohde as a soldier. This guarded view was based entirely on the rumors surrounding Rohde's older brother. Those rumors had left Rohde tainted goods in the eyes of his fellow soldiers, but the captain had given him a chance to be his own man. Fischer was pragmatic in that any good officer knew that his most important task was to make himself look good. Rohde helped him do just that.

"Why don't you shoot, for God's sake!" the captain muttered again. "He's going to make it across the field."

Rohde had come to realize that a good sniper was discon-nected from time in a way that made others impatient.

There was no hurrying a good shot, but he couldn't keep the Hauptmann waiting forever.

Rohde whistled. The noise was just loud enough for the GI to hear. It was a noise that was out of place in a field where the primary sound was the buzzing of insects.

Startled, the American pulled up short and listened. In doing so, he unwittingly presented the perfect target. He must have thought that he was hearing one of his own men signaling him. He looked in Rohde's general direction, but could not see the concealed sniper.

Rohde fired.

CHAPTER FIVE

ROHDE'S BULLET struck the GI in the leg, just above the knee. The impact raised a puff of atomized flesh and shredded olive drab uniform. He went down in the grass, thrashing in pain. Wounded, but not dead.

Fischer observed through Zeiss *Dienstglas* binoculars that would have cost two months of his officer's pay if he had not picked them up on the battlefield.

"You should have aimed a little higher," he said.

Somehow, the American managed to regain his feet. Tough bastard. He limped for the safety of the hedgerow on the opposite side of the field.

Rohde worked the bolt action, ejecting the spent round, and slapped home the bolt to lock a fresh 7.92 mm round in the chamber. In the time it took to work the bolt and reacquire the target, the GI had already moved several meters. Once again, Rohde wished for that semiautomatic rifle.

Aiming for the legs, he fired again.

This time, the GI stumbled as if someone had tripped him. He fell headlong into the grass. The bullet had gone through both legs, leaving them useless and mangled, but he tried to crawl on his elbows. Rohde watched, unconcerned. At that rate, it would take the wounded man all day to get across the field.

"What are you waiting for? You should finish him off," Fischer said, craning his head above Rohde's helmet in order to get a better view of the field.

"Please get down, sir," Rohde muttered, keeping his eye on the scope.

Fischer did not need to be told twice. He pressed his belly into the grass like he was humping the earth.

Having fired twice from the same position, Rohde's concern was that the Americans hidden in the hedgerow would return fire. When they did not, he was assured that he still remained hidden, at least for now. It was hard to pinpoint where a single shot originated, but the more times that he fired made his hiding place more obvious.

His shoulder ached dully, having taken a pounding from the K98. The rifle packed a wallop, and the bare wooden stock left a bruise after just a few rounds. Rohde had been doing a lot of shooting the last few days. Under his tunic, his shoulder and upper arm were black and blue.

Rohde's ears rang from the crack of the rifle, but as the ringing faded, he began to hear again the insects in the grass around them, unperturbed by the rifle shots. Also, he could hear the American, calling for help. It was a horrible, pleading sound. The words were in English, but they needed no translation. Rohde tuned it out, managing to ignore the fact that he was the cause of that suffering. Beside him, Captain Fischer muttered something sympathetic but did not order to finish off the American.

Keeping his scope trained on the green tangle of the hedgerow at the edge of the field, Rohde waited.

German or American, it was against human nature to

leave a wounded comrade in the middle of a field on a hot day.

The hedgerow did an excellent job of concealing the American squad hidden within it. He understood that such hedgerows were rare in America, but they were common enough in Europe. Much of the coastal countryside here in France was crisscrossed by them. The hedgerows had been most plentiful around Normandy, bogging down the Allied advance.

This patchwork of fields favored the German defensive strategy. The Allies were forced to capture France field by field. It was painstaking and deadly work.

Now, the country was more open as the fighting moved closer to Caen and Falaise, and ultimately to the Belgian border, as the Germans gave up ground, meter by meter, selling it dearly. However, much of the landscape was still comprised of small fields ringed by hedgerows, and this was where Rohde's unit had taken up a defensive position today.

The fields tended to contain no more than a few acres and were originally ringed by low stone walls. The hedgerows, made up of a medley of trees and shrubs, had grown up and over the stone walls and earthen berms. Some of the hedgerows were ancient, as he understood it, dating back to Roman times. Up to twenty feet high and almost as thick, the hedgerows eliminated the need for any fencing. Narrow sunken lanes sometimes ran between the fields, with the lanes surrounded on all sides by the hedgerows, so that traversing the countryside was almost like passing through a tunnel.

Now, Rohde kept his eyes trained on the hedgerow opposite him and waited.

The vegetation shifted. The drab green American uniforms blended effectively with the leaves and branches, but it was their movement that gave them away. He could see them shift into position, readying themselves up for action.

Rohde did not move a muscle. Every cell of his body felt like it was dipped in stone. A few more ants trooped across his neck and up under his collar. A fly landed on his cheekbone, tasting his sweat. The sun beat down. The heat was such that distant objects shimmered. He ignored the distractions, keeping his eye on the wall of vegetation. As the heat of the day increased, the insects and birds grew lazy and fell silent, so that the world seemed to be holding its breath.

Beside him, there was a sound as Fischer pulled his MP40 around and got it into position, putting the metal stock against his shoulder and bracing the weapon with his elbows. From that prone position, he would be able to sweep the field if necessary. What the MP40 lacked in range, it made up for in the quantity of 9 mm rounds it spewed out. Rohde just prayed that the captain wouldn't open fire and reveal their position to the enemy until the time was right. But an enlisted man didn't go giving orders to a Hauptmann.

Finally, there was decisive movement from the Americans. Two figures sprinted for the open field, headed for their wounded companion. Rohde tracked them through the scope. He became a little too excited by the appearance of the two targets and shot the first man through the torso, a killing shot.

He let out a breath as he worked the bolt, annoyed that he had to slap it into place. He acquired another target.

Take your time, he told himself.

He aimed lower. His next shot hit the running man, again through the legs, and he went down.

The others sheltering in the hedgerow opened fire, spewing bullets in every direction.

Beside him, Fischer cursed. He held his fire.

But the shots did not come near where they sheltered among the shrubs and grass, hugging the earth. The Americans didn't have any idea where he was hidden. When they let up off their triggers, it was possible to hear the desperate shouts of not one, but *two* wounded men in the field.

Rohde waited. The Americans knew he was there, which kept them from attempting to rescue the two men down in the field. The sun climbed higher. Sweat trickled down Rohde's face, but he didn't dare wipe it away. His mouth had gone dry and he was desperately thirsty, but he did not reach for his canteen. The slightest motion could give him away.

The sounds of the countryside gradually resumed. Insects buzzed and birds sang. Somewhere in the distance, a cow lowed. It might have been a bucolic scene if not for the fact that Rohde was watching it all through the eye of his Zeiss scope. The moans and pleas of the wounded Americans didn't help.

"This is awful to listen to," Fischer said. "Shoot them and be done with it."

Rohde weighed whether or not he should disagree with his officer. Because it was just the two of them out here, without any need for Fischer to save face, Rohde simply said, "We should wait."

Fischer sighed. "You are the sniper."

He had baited the trap. In comparison, waiting was the easy part. Rohde was prepared to stay there all day if necessary.

The afternoon wore on. To his surprise, he heard Fischer breathing deeply beside him. The captain had fallen asleep.

Rohde's bladder was getting full to the point of bursting. Tired of the distraction, and not wanting to leave his sniper's nest, he allowed himself to urinate where he lay. A puddle of warm liquid oozed out from beneath him and the smell of his own piss filled his nostrils. His bodily functions satisfied, he re-focused his full attention on the view through the tele-scopic sight.

The sun passed its zenith. The Americans lost patience.

One of them broke from the hedgerow and ran toward his wounded companions, clutching a rifle in one hand and a canteen in the other.

Rohde tracked him through the scope, leading him just a little. Then he pulled the trigger and the American fell.

He worked the bolt, shot the first wounded man. Worked the bolt, and shot the second. Beside him, Fischer jerked awake as if he'd been shot himself.

The American squad fired blindly, bullets zipping through the grass. They had not figured out where he was, but he wasn't taking any chances of getting hit by a lucky shot.

"Come on," he said to Fischer, who was still addled with sleep, and started to back away, slithering out of his position, staying on his belly. Fischer didn't need to be told twice.

They retreated until they reached another hedgerow, and buried themselves in it. Safely on the other side of the field now, they straightened up and started down the road toward where their unit was holding the line against the Allied advance.

Fischer glanced at Rohde's wet trousers and wrinkled his nose. "Uggh. You've pissed yourself," Fischer remarked.

"I can always dry out my trousers, sir." Now that they were back among the Wehrmacht forces moving on the road, he was careful to address the Hauptmann properly. "But it's not every day that I can kill Amis."

To count as a kill, each one of Rohde's victories had to be verified independently. He was glad that the Hauptmann had come along today.

Fischer shook his head. "You are collecting dead men as if they were stamps. Why are you so worried about keeping score?"

"Do I need to tell you, sir?" Rohde gave him one of those puppy grins. Even Fischer found it disarming. "You must know."

"You and your Iron Cross," Captain Fischer said. "I doubt that any of us will live long enough to see that medal pinned on you."

"You can always send it home to my family, sir," Rohde said. "In any case, that was three more for me today."

Fischer snorted. Rohde was one of the few soldiers he had ever encountered who openly lobbied for a medal. The Iron Cross was Germany's decoration for heroism on the battlefield. The medal was worn over the left pocket of the uniform tunic—over the heart. A soldier who wore the Iron Cross commanded respect.

Only one medal was more prestigious, and that was the Knight's Cross, worn at the throat. Enlisted men didn't have a chance at that.

As soon as Rohde had the sniper rifle in his hands, he had made his intentions clear that he would shoot as many of the enemy as it took to win the Iron Cross. While it was unusual for a soldier to announce that he sought to earn such a medal, in Fischer's mind it made it clear that Rohde was a committed soldier. Anyway, whatever made Rohde look good, made Fischer look good. He had done the right thing by making him the unit's *Jäger*.

Fischer clapped him on the shoulder. "You are too much, Rohde. Go get yourself something to eat." He wrinkled his nose. "And for God's sake, get out of those pants."

"Yes, sir. But first I want to swing through some of the farm country behind us and scout it out."

"Suit yourself," Fischer said. "Always hunting, aren't you, Rohde?"

With a nod, Rohde slipped off into the fields to explore some of the surrounding farms.

It did not hurt that his reconnoitering would take him past the farm of the French girl whose bed he had been sharing the past few weeks.

He wouldn't come out and say it to the Hauptmann, but it was no secret that the Germans were steadily giving up ground. What looked to be peaceful fields would soon be a battleground, and Rohde knew that knowing the ground would only work to his advantage.

When the Allied advance arrived in force, Rohde would be ready to add even more notches to his rifle stock.

CHAPTER SIX

THREE WEEKS earlier

LISETTE REMEMBERED WELL that summer day when she had met her German soldier.

"Elsa, get away from the road!" she had shouted at her niece, waving at her with a scooping gesture that was universal for "come here." The little girl ran toward her, with her twin brother, Leo, racing after her.

The two children, both five years old, had been tossing rocks into a puddle left in the dirt road by last night's rain. Already, their clothes were spattered with mud. Lisette put her hands on her hips to signal that she had lost patience. It wasn't that she was worried about the mud, but about vehicles. The road was not usually busy, but why take any chances? A speeding German motorcycle or *Kübelwagen* would not be concerned about a couple of French children getting in the way.

The children dashed toward her, their smiles and laughter

making it impossible to be angry with them. Still, caring for her niece and nephew on her own was not easy. Not a day went by that she did not wonder what it would be like to be living in Paris, with her own apartment and friends her own age, instead of isolated on this farm. Even *occupied* Paris seemed more appealing than this farm.

She sighed. "Here, you can feed the chickens instead," she said, pouring a scoop of grain into both of their hands.

The twins were soon running around the yard being chased by the chickens, eager for a handful of grain. Leo and Elsa squealed with delight.

There had been more chickens, more than a dozen, in fact, but now their flock was down to four birds. It was enough for a few eggs, but not enough for the occasional chicken dinner. Wandering German soldiers had absconded with a few chickens, but the foxes that sneaked in during the night had taken a greater toll. Without Henri there to chase them off with his battered double-barreled shotgun, the foxes had run rampant. He had left the shotgun behind, along with a handful of shells. The Germans had seized almost all guns, but they had allowed farmers to keep their shotguns. Of course, it was almost impossible to find shells anymore.

Though it was an antique, complete with hammers that had to be cocked in order to fire the weapon, she kept the shotgun cleaned and well-oiled. Henri had given her lessons in how to use it, and she had spent an afternoon firing at pumpkins to get a feel for the gun. That exercise had left her with a sore shoulder, but a bit more confidence in her marksmanship. She kept it behind the kitchen door, unloaded, with the handful of shells that remained on a high shelf where the children could not reach them.

Children to mind. Foxes to scare off. And then there was the farm work. Fences to mend. A garden to weed. The barn roof to patch. Everywhere she looked, the land seemed to threaten to take back the farm. The children were such a handful that the heavier chores around the small holding simply hadn't gotten done without Henri.

Henri. She felt a mix of pride, sadness, and resentment toward her brother. Excited by the news of the Allied landing that had finally arrived after four years of German occupation, her older brother had left that fateful June day to join the fighting, leaving his young children in her care. She had not heard from him since. Her sister in law had passed away of a fever not long after the children were born.

She loved the children dearly, but they were a great deal of work and worry.

Watching the children having their fun, it was easy enough to forget that there was a war going on. The Germans based in nearby Argentan left them alone. No one liked being an occupied nation, but the truth was that in the end there had been little to fear from the Germans. If she had been Jewish, it might be a different story, of course. She had heard the whispers and rumors.

She had little interaction with the occupiers, other than to see them passing on the road. The worst part lately had been getting enough to eat.

Lately, food had been running scarce because of the war. She worried that the twins were starting to look thin. Her own clothes felt loose.

As she went about her morning chores in the farmyard, Lisette felt lightheaded. She paused until the dizziness passed. She had skipped breakfast this morning so that the twins could eat.

She had no money to buy food, and besides that, what could she buy? The German soldiers had picked the area clean. Her nearest neighbor, Madame Pelletier, understood

Lisette's plight and was as generous as the old woman could be. She had little enough herself. Lisette's other neighbors were mostly elderly farmers who had little to share, or who were too stingy. The German occupation had not always brought out the best in the French.

She and the children moved toward the farmyard behind the cottage, where it would be safer for them to play.

Lisette rounded the corner of the cottage and froze.

A German soldier was crouched over the water pump, filling his canteen. He looked up at Lisette without any particular surprise. He must have heard her and the children nearby. Her eyes flicked to his weapon, a rifle with a telescopic sight. Considering that he seemed to be alone, and that he carried this sort of rifle, it indicated that he was one of the German's *Jäger*. In French, the formal name was *un tireur d'elite*, but the term *sniper* was mostly used. She suppressed a shudder. These *Jäger* were killers.

The children went to her and hid behind her skirts, as if sensing danger. Even they were not so young that they didn't know a German soldier was trouble.

The soldier saw her look at the rifle, but he went back to filling the canteen. Water came out in a burst when the handle was pumped, but it was not an easy task to pump the handle and then make it around to the spigot to catch the water as it came out. He was just managing. Once the canteen was full, he set it aside and took off his helmet. His hair was matted and sweaty in the heat.

He pumped the handle again and tried to get his head under the flow, but he was just a little too slow to get the full burst of water that arrived with each pump of the handle.

Thinking that it might get rid of him sooner, Lisette approached. She jerked her chin at the handle to signal that she would work the pump, and he nodded.

He stuck his head under the pump and this time, he caught the full stream of the cooling water. Even under the circumstances, Lisette had to admit how good the cascading water looked on this hot day. The soldier sighed with what sounded like relief.

His head dripping, she was surprised when he began stripping off his tunic. His skin was very pale in the sunlight. She could not help noticing that arms and chest were well-formed and muscular. She guessed that they were about the same age, although he might have been just a little younger. He raised both arms to push the hair out of his eyes, revealing blondish hair in his armpits, and she noticed that the only other hair on his body was a single patch of thatch on his chest no bigger than her hand, just where the metal disk of his *Hundermarken* dangled. She felt a bit of heat come to her cheeks. Was she actually blushing at the sight of this German boy?

Elsa pointed at his pale torso and giggled, but the soldier didn't seem to mind. Grinning now, he nodded at Lisette, indicating that she should work the pump, and he held himself under the water, taking an impromptu bath. Water ran down and soaked the waistband of his trousers. Satisfied, he straightened up and stood dripping in the barnyard. He really wasn't much more than a teenager. Sadly, Lisette suddenly remembered that she wasn't much more than a girl herself. It was a fact that she had forgotten in the face of tending to the twins and the farm. Children grew up fast these days.

"*Danke*," he said. Then, smiling at Leo and Elsa, he asked, "*Sind das deine Kinder?*"

Even after the years of occupation, Lisette knew maybe a hundred words of German. She caught the word for children.

"*C'est ma nièce et mon neveu.*"

He nodded. "*Tante.*" Aunt. The word was the same in

German and in French, although in German it seemed to be pronounced in a manner that gave it two syllables.

She nodded again.

He dressed, pulling on his soiled uniform again, although he seemed reluctant about it. Who could blame him? The sunshine must have felt so good on his pale body. He put on his ugly steel helmet and picked up the rifle. Instantly, he was transformed into a soldier once more.

For the first time, he seemed to really notice Lisette. He looked her up and down. Some sort of calculation was going on behind the soldier's blue eyes, and Lisette did not care for what she saw there. She became acutely aware of how alone and vulnerable she was here on the farm.

"*Ton père?*" the soldier asked. "*Ton mari?*"

"*Mon frere,*" she replied in French. "My brother is in the village and will be home soon."

The soldier nodded as if he understood, although it was impossible to tell. Then he patted down his pockets and produced a tin of meat and a package of crackers. He handed them to Lisette and she noticed with surprise that the food-stuffs were marked in English. Where had he gotten those?

His hand dipped into another pocket and produced a chocolate bar the size of a franc note, which he offered to the twins. The heat of the day had warmed the chocolate, and the smell of it after months without any sort of sweets was intoxi-cating. Wide-eyed, they looked to her for permission, and when she nodded, they grabbed the chocolate as ravenously as the hens had pecked at their corn. Lisette made sure that they thanked him. He might be a German, but the French still minded their manners.

"Dieter," he said, patting his damp chest.

"Lisette," she blurted out, almost by reflex.

He smiled, his blue eyes twinkling.

She felt a bit more heat touch her cheeks, then chided

herself. This was a German soldier, for God's sake. It was best to avoid any trouble.

Then the soldier turned and walked off toward the road. Before he rounded the corner of the old house, he looked back over his shoulder for a final glance at Lisette.

He gave her another smile, and then he was gone.

CHAPTER SEVEN

LISETTE MADE a feast that evening with the food the German soldier had given them. The tin contained chopped ham. The writing on the tin was in English. Where had the German obtained it? Off a dead American? She shuddered at the thought because the Americans were fighting to liberate France, but she and the children were too hungry to let her principles stop them from devouring the food.

At the thought of food, her belly rumbled painfully. It had been a long time since she had eaten a full meal. There were days when she was dizzy with hunger, having given the lion's share of her food to the twins. Henri was nowhere to be found; he seemed to have abandoned his sister and his children.

Lisette made an omelet with the tinned ham, using eggs that she had been saving, and one of the precious peppers from her garden. Together with the crackers, it was a feast, the most delicious food that they had eaten in weeks. The twins had long since given up being picky eaters. There was some wisdom in the old saying that hunger was the best sauce. Seeing the children stuff themselves pleased her to no end.

She washed the children, scrubbing off the day's dust, and put them to bed, reading them a story in an effort to drown out the distant boom of artillery. To the children, who had grown up with war, the sound was no more threatening than far away thunder on a summer evening. She kissed them and tucked them in, then retreated, gratefully, to the kitchen, where she could be blissfully alone with her thoughts.

She kept a jug of rough red wine in the cabinet, and she allowed herself a tiny glass as she sat at the table and let her mind drift.

She thought about the German soldier. *Dieter*. If anyone had asked her an hour ago, she would have answered that she hoped never to see him again. But now that she had eaten, and seen the satisfied look that full bellies brought to the twins' faces, she was not so sure of her earlier answer.

Lisette was not naive. A soldier who brought her food would expect something in return. Was she prepared to make such a trade?

She would have to be careful. More than one local girl had been shunned for what was euphemistically called "horizontal collaboration." If the Germans were forced to leave, there would be worse than shunning. Already, in places that Wehrmacht forces had abandoned, French girls who had taken German lovers were having their heads shaved, and being marched through the liberated streets in their slips, to the jeers of their old neighbors.

The question was, how far would she be willing to go to put food on the table for herself and the twins? The little flutter in her stomach when she thought of Dieter meant that she did not entirely trust herself to turn him down. He'd had a handsome face with nice eyes, and his body, though pale, had been lean and muscular.

Sipping her wine, she thought about how her life had turned out so far. It had not been so long ago that she had been excited about the possibilities. Looking back, she had dreamt of so much more. She thought again of her dreams of moving to Paris, away from the country. Then the war had broken out. With her brother gone and the children to tend, her world had grown smaller, rather than larger. Except for the children and a few old people in the village, she hardly spoke to anyone. She sighed.

Lisette was just thinking about a second, tinier glass of wine when there was a knock at the door. She froze in fear. Their old dog, too lazy to chase foxes, stirred himself from where he slept on the stone floor to bark at the door. She thought about the old shotgun, but quickly dismissed the idea. She was not expecting trouble, and she doubted that trouble would bother to knock.

She went to answer the door, half expecting it to be one of her elderly neighbors, needing help with some chore or simply wanting to complain about some ache or pain. But the quiet leading up to the knock on the door had been so stealthy. Not the shuffling of an old woman through the dark farmyard. In her heart, she already knew who it was.

She opened the door.

Standing there was the soldier from the yard. She felt a quiver of something that wasn't entirely fear.

"*Allo*," he said. His eyes went past her to search the empty kitchen.

All that Lisette could do was stare.

The German raised a sack and smiled. She could hear the shifting of tin cans inside. More food. She stepped back from the doorway to let him inside. He was not wearing his helmet, but a soft hat that the Germans called a *Schiff*. He had a fresh-scrubbed look about him, as if he had taken some pains with his appearance. He looked far different from the scruffy soldier who had cooled off at her water pump earlier that day.

The soldier entered and put the sack on the ancient, scarred wooden table. Belatedly remembering his manners, he snatched off the *Schiff*, revealing tousled blondish hair. He really was rather pretty, she thought. He certainly did not look dangerous. She let her guard down ever so slightly.

Then he sat. He nodded at another chair to indicate that she should sit as well. First, she got another glass and poured him wine.

"*Danka*," he said, smiling shyly.

The language barrier was a gap between them, but not so much a wall as a gossamer curtain. As if to fill the silence, or perhaps to make his case, the German removed items one by one from the sack. There were six more tins similar to the one that had enabled their feast tonight. More packages of crackers. Finally, two four-ounce bars of bitter Hershey's chocolate, which he added to the top of the stack, like a finishing touch. Altogether, the food made up what was known to American GIs as a D ration.

She thanked him, although she was unable to take her eyes off the food. There was so much of it.

They sat for another few moments in silence. He smiled, and Lisette returned the smile. Then the German stood. He reached down and took her hand, guiding Lisette to her feet. She thought that he might try to kiss her, but instead, his eyes flicked toward the narrow hallway. The one that led toward her bedroom.

She understood then why the German had brought her food. It was a simple transaction. An unspoken deal had been struck. Now, she realized that she must live up to her end of the bargain if she and the children wanted to eat.

Her heart pounding, she led the way to her bed.

* * *

SINCE THAT FIRST NIGHT, the German had been a frequent visitor. He always brought food, for which Lisette was grateful. The twins were thin enough that the extra food was welcome to supplement what little came from the farm.

Alone for the moment, with the twins tucked into their beds and the old dog lounging at her feet, she sat at the battered kitchen table and poured a tiny glass of the rough red wine. This quiet time had become a ritual, and her favorite time of the day.

It was now August. As it grew dark, she lit an oil lantern. The cottage was close enough to the main road to have electricity and even a telephone, but sometimes she preferred the warm glow of the old-fashioned lamp. A moth appeared and bumped in futility against the glass globe of the lantern, intent on destroying itself in the flame. In the distance, she could hear the ominous thump of artillery, still many miles distant, but louder than it had been in days past. The flashes on the horizon resembled the heat lightning present when a storm was gathering.

She thought about Dieter. If the German was using her, no matter; she was using him as well. Lisette had been surprised to make this discovery about herself, that she had the capacity to use and to be used, but instead of being disappointed in herself, she took a small measure of pride in the fact that she was being practical and tough. It was enough that she loved the twins with all her heart; she did not need to love the German. Not that she minded having him in her bed.

She did not know how this affair would end. She just assumed that one day, the German boy would simply not return, having been caught up in the maelstrom of war. She suspected that the German forecast this as well. As a result, they both seemed to savor each caress, each coupling in the dark, each sip of wine and bite of contraband food, all the more. They were both on borrowed time. They did not need to speak one another's language to understand that they dwelt together like two castaways in a lifeboat, drifting in an eddy of the current on a rushing river.

Soon enough, the tide would rush even faster and sweep everything away.

Lisette finished her wine, then raised the globe of the lamp, allowing the moth to come to its fiery end.

CHAPTER EIGHT

HIDDEN in the hayloft of the barn, lying prone on the dusty wooden floorboards, Rohde was immobile as a snake. He had been there since before dawn, keeping watch over the field as the shadows gave way to day under gray skies. So far, there had been no movement of American troops through the summer grass.

For a moment, his mind drifted. He thought of his dead brother, Carl. Sometimes, he carried on a conversation with Carl as a way to pass the time on these lonely sniper hunts.

You would like it here in France, Carl, Rohde thought. In the early morning quiet, up under the rafters of the barn, it almost seemed as if he had spoken his thoughts out loud. *The countryside is so peaceful. It reminds me of when we used to hunt rabbits when we were boys. You always thought that you were the better shot, but look at me now. Those rabbits would not stand a chance, Carl!*

The report of a rifle snapped him back to the present. That would be Scheider. The other sniper had placed himself in a copse of trees just to the west of the barn, in order to hold up the movement of American troops on the road that lay just beyond the hedgerow bordering Rohde's field.

Rodhe had talked with Scheider just that morning before sunrise. Their unit had been there for a few weeks now, and the cooks had settled in, preparing hearty breakfasts from sausages and eggs. It seemed hard to believe that was possible, with the Allies closing in, but here was the delicious-smelling evidence on his plate.

Now that the American advance had reached this deep into France, the makeshift kitchen would soon be closed, along with the regular offerings of fresh-baked bread and fresh eggs from the surrounding countryside. There was even the occasional offering of ham or bacon.

French patriotism only went so far, it seemed. Local farmers were eager for a bit of cash or to trade for coffee or other supplies, although there would be hell to pay for trading with the enemy once the Germans cleared out and the vengeful *Machi* forces took over. They were all Communists—no better than the Russians. But for now, the field kitchen was still in operation, and Rohde stuffed himself in preparation for a long day of action.

"Hunting again, eh, Rohde? Where are you off to today?" Scheider had asked him around 4 a.m., when they had both run into one another, getting a cup of coffee at the field kitchen set up in a barn.

"Here and there," Rohde said, not wanting to reveal too much. If he had any rival as a sniper and *Jäger*, it was Scheider. Short and sturdy, Scheider had once told him that he had grown up in the farm country around Munich, hunting and shooting. He was an excellent shot. Fortunately for Rohde, Hauptmann Fischer evidently found it hard to relate to the earthy farm boy. Scheider himself seemed oblivious to any sense of rivalry. He cut two thick slices of bread and handed one to Rohde.

Unbidden, a plan came to mind for how he might use Scheider.

"Have you thought about trying your luck on the road to Saint Dennis de Mere?" Rohde asked.

A light seemed to go on behind Scheider's eyes. "That is a good plan. Easy pickings. I spotted a copse of trees at a bend in the road yesterday. Perhaps I will set up shop there, unless you were thinking of it."

"No, no, you go ahead. You would give the Amis quite a surprise," Rohde said as nonchalantly as possible.

"How many did you get yesterday?"

"Six," Rohde said.

Scheider gave a low whistle as he layered butter on his slice of bread. "If I set up on the road maybe I will get that many today. Or more."

"Maybe so."

"Are you sure you don't mind?" Scheider laughed good-naturedly. "You had better watch out, or I will beat your record!"

"Good luck with that," Rohde said as genially as possible, although Scheider's words made him nervous. He moved off to fill his plate.

He tended to eat by himself. No one but a fellow *Jäger* like Scheider was much interested in conversation at four o'clock in the morning. Rohde had found that he liked the time alone, to focus his thoughts for the day. Anyhow, nobody was all that eager to break bread with a man they saw as a lone wolf.

After breakfast, he walked out to the latrine to evacuate his bowels. He had trained himself to make that basic bodily function part of his morning routine. He did not want to be caught in the field needing to relieve himself.

He thought about what Scheider had said about breaking

his record. Though spoken in jest, perhaps Scheider planned to knock Rohde off his pedestal as a sniper. The very idea that anyone might be pulling ahead of Rohde was worrisome.

All that Rohde could think about was that Iron Cross. He wanted that medal. He *needed* that medal. Nobody was going to stop him, least of all a farm boy like Scheider.

That medal is for us, Carl, he thought.

With any luck, that farm boy was going to help him shoot a few Amis today, whether Scheider knew it or not.

Rohde knew that copse of trees well enough, along with the surrounding countryside. In his mind's eye, he could picture the Americans stacking up on the road, bottlenecked by the sniper.

What would they do? If they had a Sherman tank, they would reduce the copse to splinters, along with Scheider. The trick was to fire into the treetops and shatter the branches, amplifying a single shell burst into a thousand deadly oak splinters.

Without support from a tank, the Americans would move off the road into the field in an effort to flank the sniper. They would probably move into the field to the north, which would give them a better approach to the wood where Scheider would be positioned.

Rohde thought about a squad moving into the field. He could pick them off at random. There was an old barn that, if memory served, would be an ideal location from which to shoot. The barn would offer protection and height.

At first light, Rohde was there, waiting.

He had ascended the ladder into the loft. He had found some old sleigh bells and draped them over the ladder leading up to the loft. He would be alerted instantly if anyone tried the ladder.

Again, his mind wandered to his brother. *A good sniper*

hide, Carl. Though I would not mind something warm to drink. Isn't it supposed to be summer? The mornings are still cold.

Then Rohde settled down to wait for someone to enter his killing field.

CHAPTER NINE

HAVING JUST COME FROM HEADQUARTERS, Lieutenant Mulholland approached with purpose in his stride.

"Hey, Cole," he shouted, still on the move. "Get your hill-billy ass over here."

The lieutenant had directed his shout toward a handful of GIs sprawled in the grass, limp as rag dolls with exhaustion. Lack of sleep, the heat and humidity, and constant exertion had left them worn out. Their uniforms had white salt stains from constant sweating. Their grimy appearance and ragged uniforms underscored the fact that they had all become battle-hardened warriors since coming ashore two months before. The war now seemed like all that they had ever known.

Unlike the other men prostrate in the grass, Cole rested on his haunches as if ready to spring into action at any moment. The others had put down their weapons, but a rifle with a telescopic sight was balanced across his knees. Cole's grayish eyes flicked toward the lieutenant, simultaneously alert and disinterested, like the glance of a predator that was sizing you up as prey.

Mulholland's forward momentum stopped at the sight of those eyes.

Cole said, "Yeah?"

"I just heard from headquarters. They've got a job for you."

Cole got to his feet, not so much standing, as uncoiling. He didn't ask what the job involved. Cole was a sniper. Nobody was going to ask him to change a tire or type a report.

"The 118th is running up against a sniper," the lieutenant explained. "A goddamn good one. He shot three guys yesterday."

"Three, huh? Maybe he got lucky."

"That's three in *one day*, Cole. Just as many the day before. And the day before that."

Cole exhaled through his teeth, making a thin whistle. "I reckon that's a lot of marks on the stock of his Mauser."

"That's where you come in. You need to take that Mauser and shove it up his ass."

Cole's grin left a chill along the lieutenant's spine, even in the heat of the French summer. Not for the first time, he was glad that Cole was on his side.

"I reckon I can do that." He turned to look at Vaccaro, who usually teamed up with Cole as his spotter. Vaccaro also carried a rifle with a telescopic sight, but at the moment, both the rifle and its owner lay stretched out in the grass. "You up for this, City Boy?"

Vaccaro opened one eye and shook his head. "Goddammit, Cole. Why do you always have to volunteer me for this shit?"

"Suit yourself." Cole turned away.

Vaccaro rolled to a sitting position and reached for his rifle. "C'mon, Cole. Don't get a stick up your ass. All I'm saying is that some of us want a break now and then."

Cole was already walking away, so Vaccaro hurried to catch up.

"I thought you weren't comin'?"

"I don't even know why you want me along, Hillbilly. I'd almost think you were lonely, if you weren't the most solitary individual I've run across. Next time, let me sleep unless you need help with the rough stuff. You know this is just some German kid who got lucky with a rifle."

"You sure about that?" Cole didn't believe that the German sniper he was being sent to dispatch was simply lucky. Luck ran out; anyone who had lasted several days as a sniper with any success had skill, and skill was far more worrisome. Skill got you killed. "Anybody gets lucky once in a while, City Boy, but not three days in a row. This German knows his business."

Having gotten his orders, Cole set off toward where the lieutenant had told him the German sniper was operating. Vaccaro trailed along, grumbling under his breath. Cole had heard it all before, so he ignored him.

Cole had no doubt that somebody was needed to settle this German's hash, but the truth was that he did not trust Lieutenant Mullholland's motives one hundred percent. Mulholland could have sent another sniper—hell, he could have sent Vaccaro—but he had singled out Cole. From a young age, Cole had been schooled to expect the worst from people.

Few people acted out of goodness. The Army hadn't taught him any different.

While Mulholland was mostly trustworthy, it was also true that he and the lieutenant had some baggage. It was the kind of thing that went unsaid, but it was there all the same. Just a few weeks before, they had both fallen for a certain member of the French Resistance named Jolie Molyneaux.

She had been assigned as their scout through the *bocage*

countryside around Normandy. From her role in the Resistance, Jolie knew the paths and trails through that maze of hedgerows and fields.

She had been more than capable, but they had run into some trouble along the way. Cole had found himself in a duel with a German sniper, one of the best there was, and had barely come out of it alive.

Jolie hadn't gotten off so easy. She was still recuperating in a field hospital after being shot by the German. Mulholland was not only jealous that Jolie had preferred Cole, but he blamed Cole for Jolie being shot.

The way Cole saw things, it was the German's fault that Jolie had been shot. He was the one who had been doing the shooting. But that wasn't how Mulholland saw it. He blamed Cole for putting her in harm's way. He had this chivalrous idea that women didn't belong in a combat zone. Never mind the fact that Jolie was a damn good fighter.

Cole hated to think that the lieutenant had some ulterior motive, hoping that Mulholland might be the exception to the rule, but it seemed to him that missions like this were payback. Mulholland had volunteered him. While it was true that Cole was more likely than others to solve the sniper problem, it was a good bet that in Mulholland's book it would be a bonus if Cole got his ass shot off in the process.

He doubted that anyone at headquarters would have asked for him by name. Or had they? None other than the well-known journalist Ernie Pyle had written a story about him a couple of weeks before. Everyone had seemed impressed by the famous reporter and the story that he had written.

Because Cole couldn't read, he had to take everybody's word that it was a good story. So far, he had managed to keep his illiteracy a secret. He didn't mind if everybody thought he was a hillbilly, which he was, but he didn't like being seen as ignorant. One of these days, he promised himself that he would get some book learning. Until then, he had developed a few tricks to hide the fact that he couldn't read, although Vaccaro was starting to suspect the truth.

Cole loped along a country road that overflowed with soldiers. Vaccaro's gait was lumbering, but he didn't have any trouble keeping up. A city boy was used to walking fast. But while Vaccaro put his whole body into moving fast, swinging his arms for momentum with his rifle slung over one shoulder, Cole's legs seemed to glide over the landscape while his upper body held itself still, rifle always ready in his arms.

Most of the troops they passed were on the move toward some destination defended by German soldiers. Many more men lounged in the shade, smoking cigarettes and sipping warm water from aluminum canteens. Some just stared into the distance, so dazed by the endless threat of combat and by the rough conditions that they were not much better off than walking scarecrows. Here and there a man was busy scribbling a letter home, knowing full well that it might be his last.

Their rifles drew a few stares, not all of them friendly. Snipers were not exactly beloved—no soldier liked the idea of death being delivered from a distance, and snipers had a reputation for picking men off in their more vulnerable moments: having a smoke, taking a leak, trying to catch a glimpse above a wall or around a corner.

Death that came in the form of a mortar shell or a burst of machine-gun fire was awful and frightening, but it was also anonymous. Death from a sniper, someone who had picked out and targeted a single man, was far more personal, not to mention sly and sneaky.

The sniper from your own side was tolerated; a sniper from the other side seldom made it to the rear if captured.

Cole ignored the looks he was getting, and took stock of the situation.

The 118th occupied what could loosely be called the left flank, which in this case was to the northeast. Wouldn't be hard to find. If he missed the unit somehow, he'd know, because he would run smack dab into the Germans instead. The countryside was crawling with Kraut troops—Wehrmacht, Waffen SS, even Panzers.

Cole wasn't in a hurry to see a Panzer again anytime soon. There was nothing quite like the sight of a Panzer to turn your guts to water.

Vaccaro spoke up. "You know what? We could always go back and say that we couldn't find the 118th. We can just sit in the shade for a while and then head back. The lieutenant won't be any the wiser."

"Mulholland won't believe us," Cole said. "All we got to do is follow the sound of shooting."

Cole was right—to a point.

The lines changed daily because control of the surrounding countryside was in flux. While the Germans were steadily being pushed back by the overwhelming numbers of Allied forces, they sold each inch of ground dearly.

It didn't help the situation that other Allied forces were part of the mix: Brits, Canadians, the vicious and undisciplined French Resistance, even elements of the free Polish Army. There was enough confusion among American troops, let alone troops with soldiers who spoke their own brand of English, or none at all. Officers of different nationalities were eager to have their troops drive the farthest each day, for their personal and national glory. The sense of competition outweighed cooperation.

The situation was ripe for what GIs called a SNAFU—

Situation Normal, All Fouled Up. Friendly fire incidents were becoming more common.

Cole didn't much like the idea of getting shot by his own side. The Germans were enough to worry about.

CHAPTER TEN

FORTUNATELY, Cole and Vaccaro found the 118th before they found any trouble of the Kraut variety. Like every American GI in France, these guys looked haggard and worn out. Like Cole, they wore the same M41 Style Field Jackets they had come ashore with weeks before. Though durable, the densely woven cotton fabric was now stained, ripped, and filthy. Nobody had showered or shaved in days.

They barely looked up as Cole and Vaccaro appeared with their sniper rifles. Again, Cole was reminded that soldiers on both sides had mixed emotions about snipers. At best, there was a mystique about snipers. They were held apart from an ordinary rifleman because of their skill and special equipment. At worst, they were seen as sneaky sons of bitches, and disliked accordingly.

"Who's in charge of this here goat fuck?" Cole asked, and followed the pointed fingers until he found a young captain crouched over a map.

The captain flicked his eyes over Cole's face, and then at the rifle.

"I understand that you're here to solve our sniper prob-lem," the captain said. "Fight fire with fire, right?"

Cole was immediately taken aback by the officer's Boston accent, so different from his own that it was difficult to fathom that they both came from the same country.

"Yes, sir."

"Here's the situation, Cole. We need to get up this road toward Saint Dennis de Mere. Only there's a German sniper who has set up shop in those trees up ahead. We could go around him, but it's not exactly convenient." He waved a hand in the vague direction of the fields beyond. The road was hemmed in by hedges and fences. "For all we know, the Krauts may have planted mines. This road is the most direct route, and we've got a schedule to keep."

Cole looked to where the officer was pointing. Sure enough, there was a bend in the road ahead, where the road passed around a copse of trees. The sniper had hidden in those trees, and from that vantage point now commanded the road. It was a textbook example of how a single sniper could delay an infantry unit as effectively as a tank.

Cole considered his options. Continuing down the road would be suicide. Anyone who left cover would instantly be in the sniper's sights.

He would be another dead man among many.

He thought about the sniper in the trees. Having grown up hunting and trapping in the mountains he had learned to think like the game he was stalking. It might seem silly, the idea that he could get inside the head of a deer, or a bear, and predict what that animal would do, or where he would go. But Cole could. It was what made him a good hunter—that, and being a damn good shot.

Most animals did the expected because they followed their instincts. Their brains followed a road map to get them through various situations. Humans weren't all that different.

What would the German sniper do? Bide his time and wait. If the Americans attempted a full-on assault, the German could simply slip away—after inflicting severe losses. It was more than likely that the sniper was hidden in one of the treetops, which would offer a better vantage point. The disadvantage for the German sniper was that a tree could also become a trap.

The way Cole saw it, the possibility that he could tree that sniper like a 'coon was the best he could hope for.

Cole looked at Vaccaro. "Hounds and foxes?"

Vaccaro groaned. "You and your goddamn hillbilly games. You know I hate hounds and foxes."

The captain was looking at them like headquarters had maybe sent him a couple of nut cases. "Hounds and foxes? What the hell has that got to do with anything? I've got a sniper holding up my squad, soldier."

"Don't worry, sir," Vaccaro said. "It's a strategy that me and Cole here use. Hounds chase foxes, you know. We'll make the fox think we're chasing him, but meanwhile, there's a lone hound sneaking up on the sly."

"Lone wolf," Cole corrected him. "That'd be me, sir."

The captain shook his head. "Snipers. You're in a three-way tie for crazy with paratroopers and combat engineers."

"Thank you, sir," Vaccaro said. "That means a lot."

Cole turned to the captain. "All right, here's what I'm fixin' to do. I'm a gonna get off this here road and into this field right here—" in Cole's accent, the last two words sounded like *rye cheer* "—and work my way toward them trees. In exactly ten minutes, you hit them woods with everything you got. Vaccaro will stick with you and try to get a shot from the road. Ya'll are the hounds, you see. I'll be sneaking up on him on the sly. If Vaccaro don't get him, then I'll see where he's at when he shoots back."

The captain glanced at his type A-11 Army-issue watch,

manufactured in Waltham, Massachusetts. Checking the alignment of the white hands on the black face, he said, "Ten minutes. You got it."

Taking a cue from the captain, Vaccaro checked his own watch. Or rather, watches. He had three strapped to his wrist. Spoils of war.

Their plan agreed upon, Cole eased his way into the field, careful not to attract any attention from the enemy sniper. To help create a diversion, Vaccaro took a couple of potshots at the German's position.

Cole chose the field to the north because his view of the copse of trees would not be blocked by the elbow in the road. This way he was traveling around the point of the elbow, rather than being caught in the crook. The countryside was more open here and the field reflected that, being mostly a wide-open expanse that stretched toward a distant line of trees. At one edge of the field, maybe two hundred yards away, was an ancient stone barn. Perfect cover for a sniper. Cole eyed the barn warily, but it appeared empty. There was a stillness about the structure. The only German around was in those woods, blocking the road ahead.

He crept forward.

Throughout the field were large boulders that generations of farmers had failed to move, allowing the scrub brush to grow up around them. Farmers back home did the same. These formed islands of vegetation in the cultivated field, which was otherwise knee-high with barley.

He slung the rifle so that it hung across his front, then got down on his hands and knees and started to crawl. The damp earth soaked his knees. Bits of stubble from last fall's crop jabbed into his hands. His plan was to reach one of those islands of stone and brush. From there, he would have a good vantage point toward the cluster of trees that hid the German sniper, and he would have some cover of his own.

Cole hit a patch of briers that snagged his trousers and stubbornly wouldn't let go. He got hung up and freed himself only by using his hands to pull away the brier canes. It hurt like fire, and his hands came away bloody. He kept moving.

Before he could get into position, shooting started on the road. Damn, but that captain was punctual. It sure didn't seem like ten minutes. Cole never bothered to wear a wristwatch—what good did it do for a sniper to watch the time pass? Not only that, but the glint of a crystal watch face had fatally betrayed more than one soldier. He had warned Vaccaro about that, but the damn fool city boy wouldn't listen.

Cole stopped crawling and got ready to shoot. He would have liked to make it to one of those islands of rock and brush to find a solid rest for his rifle, plus some cover, but he was out of time. The hounds were already busy shooting.

He had to shoot now, while the sniper was distracted.

He would have preferred firing from a prone position, but the vegetation blocked his view. A sitting position was his only option. He sat Indian-style, but kept his ankles as flat to the ground as possible. He hooked the sling through his right arm to help steady the Springfield, and then put his elbows over his knees, not bone to bone because that would be unsteady, but meat to meat and sinew to sinew. He bent forward at the waist, getting right up on the scope.

FROM THE BARN, Rohde watched the American sniper with professional interest.

It was past mid-morning when Rohde had heard an American squad exchange fire with Scheider, and probably getting the worst of it. That Scheider was a good shot, damn him. He ended up pinning down the squad to the point that they bunched up on the road.

Rohde was just beginning to think that his plan wasn't going to work. The Americans were being stubborn. Instead of trying to flank Scheider, and moving into Rohde's killing field, they were shooting it out on the road.

Again, to pass the time, he addressed his dead brother. *The American strategy is always to move forward. They never think about moving sideways.*

That's when he had noticed the other sniper. A flicker of motion caught his eye. *Wait. Carl, what was that?*

Rohde fixed his eyes straight ahead, relaxing his focus so that his eyes would naturally detect any movement in the field. *There.* Quickly, his sharp eyes went to the motion. It was not the entire squad moving to flank Scheider. Just one man. One with a telescopic sight on his rifle. An American sniper, which was something of an unusual sight.

Rohde felt his heart beat faster. A sniper would be a rare prize.

Captain Fischer might even put Rohde in for a medal sooner, rather than later.

After he killed this sniper, he would go down and take his rifle. Maybe the American weapon would be better than this *Stück Müll* fat old Hohenfeldt had given him.

Studying the sniper through the telescopic sight, Rohde saw a lean man who moved with the stealth of an animal, belly low to the ground. The American had something painted on his helmet. It looked like a flag of some sort.

Rohde pressed his eye closer to the sight, straining to see across the distance. The flag appeared to be a red rectangle traversed by a blue St. Andrew's X-shaped cross, with stars inside the cross. It looked a bit like the flag of Norway, as a matter of fact, but Rohde was sure that he had never seen this particular flag before. What in hell? Maybe it was a unit designation of some sort. This sniper wouldn't have been the first American to decorate his helmet in some way. In much the same manner, the Americans were always drawing pictures on their tanks and planes, and giving them silly names.

Germans saw that as akin to defacing military equipment. No tank commander in the 5th Panzer would ever decorate his Tiger tank with a picture of a half-naked woman. Who would even consider such a travesty?

Rohde let the American belly crawl through the field, knowing that he could take him at any instant. That thought made him tingle down to his boots with what was almost a sexual feeling of anticipation. *Strange, isn't it, Carl, to have the power of life and death over someone without him knowing it?* He watched with professional interest as the sniper got into a sitting position and aimed toward the copse of trees that hid Scheider.

It was all Rohde could do not to snort at the sniper's confidence. The American was a long way from where Scheider was hidden. Did the American really think he could shoot accurately from that distance? With a sitting stance, no less?

* * *

COLE SCANNED THE TREETOPS.

Down the road, bullets *snicked* at the tree branches hiding the German, but the sniper managed to return fire, keeping the Americans pinned down.

He glimpsed a burst of something deep in the shadows among the trees. It could have been a muzzle blast, or maybe just a sudden movement.

With a mental image locked in place of where he had spotted the movement, he fired. Worked the bolt, sending a brass .30/06 shell spinning away. Acquired the woodsy patch where he had seen a ripple of movement. Fired again.

The sniper in the woods fell silent.

* * *

AS ROHDE WATCHED, the sniper fired, and the shooting in the copse of trees fell silent. To hit Scheider at such a distance, this American must be a sniper of some skill.

Rohde was more than a little impressed. Rohde was glad that he had not been the one in the enemy's sights. One shot from the American and Rohde's problem with his rival was solved.

In payment, Rohde would kill the American quickly. He lined up the sight on the back of the American's helmet. The bullet would take him square in the back of the head.

Rohde held his breath and squeezed the trigger.

* * *

COLE SHIFTED to get a better look through the scope and in the next instant something inside his skull went *whang*.

He just had time to think, "Who in the hell hit me in the head with an ax handle?"

Then everything went black.

* * *

WHEN ROHDE FIRED, two things had happened as instantaneously as the primer igniting the powder in the cartridge. First, Rohde felt the satisfying jolt against his shoulder of the Mauser's recoil. In the same instant, the American cocked his head.

The American had gone down, but because the sniper had

moved just as Rohde had fired, he couldn't tell if the bullet had struck true.

He ejected the spent shell and slapped the bolt into place. The rifle jolted out of position, and he wasted precious seconds repositioning the weapon.

Hop, hop, hop. It was like he could hear his old training instructor shouting into his ear. *Hurry, hurry, hurry.*

Feeling rushed and nervous, Rohde got off another shot too quickly, because it kicked up dirt near the American's head. He took a deep breath. *Take it easy,* he told himself. The American wasn't moving. Maybe that first bullet had done for him.

He lined up the sight right between the sniper's shoulder blades.

CHAPTER ELEVEN

WHEN COLE CAME to twenty seconds later, he found himself staring at the blue summer sky, wondering what the hell had just happened.

He knew that he'd been shot. Somehow, he was still alive. His head was ringing, but there didn't seem to be any blood.

He tried to piece together the last few seconds before he'd been knocked out, hoping that it would give him some clue as to the shooter's location.

Cole had been listening for the sniper in the copse to shoot again, not sure that he'd hit him. He had tilted his head to hear better.

Just at that instant, the bullet grazed his helmet. The shot had not come from the direction of the copse, but from behind him. Cole realized that if he hadn't happened to turn his head just then, the bullet would have drilled through his skull.

Much later, when he'd had time to think on it, he reckoned that maybe he had somehow heard that bullet coming for him, outrunning sound itself. His pa had always said that he'd been born with eyes in the back of his head. It was damn near the only nice thing the old man had ever had to say about him.

Even with a glancing blow, all that energy still rattled his skull enough to knock him out for a few seconds.

The M1 helmet issued to U.S. troops since April 1941 was comprised of 2.85 pounds of steel alloy, shaped to encase the skull in a protective layer of metal that was a uniform one-eighth of an inch thick. Made by the McCord Radiator and Manufacturing Company, the helmet was famously tough and could be used for everything from a trenching tool to a hammer for tent stakes and even a cooking pot if the need arose, although this last use was discouraged because intense heat made the metal too brittle to withstand shrapnel. There were even rumors that a sergeant outside the town of Bienville had snapped and used his helmet to beat a captured SS officer to death. This use, also, was officially discouraged.

Tough and multifunctional as a helmet was, it could not stop a round from a Mauser K98.

Cole had gotten his bell rung good and proper, although his head had not actually *rung* like a bell. No, that was far too poetic a way of putting it. The sound inside his skull was more like what you heard when a sledgehammer pounded a rock.

Mountain people had a saying for being in a bad situation. *I'd jest as soon be in hell with my back broke.* That was about how he felt just then in the middle of a field, in some Kraut sniper's sights, his head full of shattering rocks.

The sniper wasn't done with him. Another bullet kicked up the dirt inches from Cole's face. *Aw, hell.*

His only chance was to find some cover. The nearest option was one of those big rocks that the farmer had plowed around.

While that made some kind of sense to his scrambled brain, his body itself seemed unwilling to move.

But it was move or die.

He began to count.

One. Two. Three—

* * *

ROHDE COULD NOT BELIEVE that he had missed his second shot.

Willing himself to take his time and make the next shot a killing one, Rohde steadied his breathing. His heart still hammered with excitement, however, which did not help his aim.

He was angry with himself for missing not once, but twice. What kind of *Dummkopf* did that? He would not be putting that in his report to Captain Fischer when he brought him the American sniper's rifle as a trophy.

What made him even more uncomfortable was knowing that he himself could be in some unseen enemy's sights. The business of sniping was multi-layered in that you never knew who was watching, or who was creeping up behind you. It was like chess; you thought that you were thinking two moves ahead, but your opponent was three moves ahead. Checkmate.

The thought was enough to make him pull his eye back from the scope and tilt his head to listen. Was it possible that the soldier in the field was some sort of decoy to distract him while others crept into the barn? His ears rang from the two shots, but even so, he would have heard any telltale sounds from the barn below.

The sleigh bells he had hung on the ladder remained silent.

Reassured that he was still alone in the barn, he pressed his eye once more to the scope.

He wasn't sure how hard the American was hit. Was the American sniper dying or simply dazed?

One more shot would settle that question.

He had to make it count. He kept the post sight settled right between the American's shoulder blades.

Rohde took in a breath, held it, and let his finger take up tension on the trigger.

* * *

AT THAT MOMENT three hundred feet away, Cole coiled his arms and legs under him and sprang up out of the grass, running like hell.

He dodged and weaved like a jackrabbit.

He heard a shot, but kept going. He knew exactly how long it took to work the bolt action of a rifle and aim again because he had done it himself hundreds of times.

One Mississippi.

Two Mississippi.

When he got to three, he juked sideways.

The bullet passed through the air that Cole's body would have occupied a fraction of a second longer.

The sound was enough to turn his legs to rubber, but he kept running, jack rabbiting it as he went. The big rock with the brush around it was just ahead.

One Mississippi.

Two Mississippi.

He gave himself until three Mississippi and dove for cover, glad to get a thick boulder and brush between himself and the shooter.

The fact that the German sniper held his fire told Cole that he'd made it. The rock wasn't any bigger than he was, so

Cole willed himself to shrink into the surrounding brush. He sunk down, panting hard.

Winded, heart hammering, skull ringing, Cole kept his head down and bunched his knees up to his chin. He wasn't aware that the only part of him showing was a patch of his left shoulder that didn't quite fit behind the rock.

CHAPTER TWELVE

IN THE BARN, Rohde watched in disbelief as his first shot missed when the American leaped up. He worked the bolt, tried to hold the sight on the running man, and fired just as the American danced to the left. He fired and missed. He was still getting the sights lined up when the soldier dived into the brush surrounding a rocky place in the field.

The rock was hardly bigger than a bushel basket, but it was enough to give the sniper cover. Rohde muttered a curse, then noticed a bit of khaki-colored uniform showing above the rock. It was hard to tell just what he was looking at—part of an arm, maybe, or maybe a shoulder.

Rohde set his sights on that target and fired.

* * *

WHEN THE GERMAN sniper in the barn fired again, Cole felt the bullet strike like somebody punching him in the arm. His body went numb at the impact and he hugged the shelter of the rock, willing his body to shrink behind it. Then the pain began, the searing agony of a million raw nerve endings.

Cole had not been shot before. The closest approximation he could imagine to what he felt now was having someone drive a hot railroad spike into his upper arm.

He couldn't decide if he was scared, or just pissed off. Maybe a little of both. What he did know what that it hurt like hell.

Trying not to move more than necessary, Cole inspected the damage. Despite the pain, one glance told him that he was lucky. The bullet had cut a groove into the flesh and muscle of his upper left arm, almost like a slash. Blood ran down his arm and puddled in the humus of decayed leaves. Within a few minutes, the worst of the bleeding stopped.

Still, it hurt like a son of a bitch.

He knew he ought to shoot back. He knew that he *had* to shoot back. But the truth was, that he was spooked. His mind told his arms to raise the rifle, put the scope to his eye, and look for a target. But his body would not obey.

He froze up.

His mind was still going, though. He thought about the fact that his shoulder hadn't exactly been a big target.

Maybe the German had just gotten lucky.

Or, maybe the sniper in the barn was that damn good.

* * *

ROHDE WATCHED CAREFULLY FOR MOVEMENT, but when he saw none, he relaxed his grip on the rifle and eased away from the gable window of the barn. He doubted that he had killed the American, but neither was the American going to forget him anytime soon.

That was a damn fine shot, he heard his dead brother's voice say.

That one was for you, Carl. I wanted to prove that the Rohde brothers are true soldiers.

Now, Rohde considered his options. He could wait to finish off the American, or he could move on. Staying in any one location for too long was a death sentence. He was already spooked by the thought of more Americans creeping into the barn. Time to go.

Where else would he hunt today? Yesterday he had done well and added several notches to the stock of his K98, but that was yesterday; today was a new day. A new opportunity.

He listened again for the sound of any intruders creeping up on him, but could only hear the birds twittering on, busy with the business of gathering food, mating, and raising their young, oblivious to the politics and ambitions of humankind. Survival was enough. Rohde understood.

Rohde crept back down the ladder and out of the barn, slipping away into the woods and fields, moving in the opposite direction from where he had last seen any American troops.

If he wanted an Iron Cross, he had to survive to hunt another day.

* * *

No more than a few minutes had passed since he'd been grazed in the head, but it felt like an eternity to Cole.

He kept his eye on the road, wondering if the American squad had moved off. What about Vaccaro?

His question was answered when he saw a figure emerge through the same hole in the hedge that he had used. If that sniper was still in the barn, and Vaccaro walked out into the field, he would be a dead man.

* * *

OUT ON THE ROAD, Vaccaro heard that lone shot from the field to his right. His first thought was, *sniper*. Nobody else took just one shot.

He knew that Cole was out there, but that had not been Cole's rifle. It was funny how after a while, he had gotten to where he could recognize the particular report that the Springfield made.

"Looks like your buddy got him," the captain said, nodding in the direction of the road ahead.

"Yeah, that's what it looks like." Vaccaro was distracted by another shot from the field, then another. Definitely not Cole's rifle. The shots were spaced out, indicating that the shooter was taking time to aim.

"We're going to advance," the captain said. "Our orders are to occupy Saint Dennis de Mere, and I'd like to do that by nightfall. You coming with us?"

"No, I'm gonna wait for Cole," Vaccaro said.

"Suit yourself," the captain said. "I've got to tell you, though, that this whole area is still crawling with Krauts."

"Thanks for the warning," Vaccaro said. "We'll try to take a few out."

"Good luck, soldier. And thanks. You and your buddy saved our bacon."

The captain gave the signal, and the squad began to move out. With the sniper in the copse of trees ahead silenced, there was nothing to impede their advance.

Vaccaro watched them go, and then turned his attention to the field beyond the road. What the hell was going on out there?

Cole had made his way through a gap in the hedgerow, and Vaccaro started to follow. He was just emerging into the field when a shot came out of nowhere and struck the dirt nearby, causing him to dive for cover.

No way was he going into that field now.

Unless he was mistaken, that had been Cole's rifle. He recognized the familiar crack of the Springfield. So now Cole was shooting at him. What the hell?

* * *

COLE HAD FIRED a couple of feet above Vaccaro's head, causing him to scramble for shelter. He just hoped that Vaccaro got the message to stay clear.

Cole bided his time, ignoring the pain in his shoulder as best he could. Another couple of inches to the right and that bullet would've blown his head clean off.

Damned if it didn't hurt, but all in all he was damn lucky. Of course, it would've been even luckier if he hadn't gotten shot at all.

Was the German sniper still in the barn? He had no way of knowing, so he waited.

Despite the summer day, he began to feel chilled laying in the shadows in the damp field. He finished the water in his canteen, but it wasn't enough. What he would have given for another drink of water.

Now he knew how a wounded animal felt, gone to ground.

He wrapped his hands firmly around his rifle, and dozed to escape the pain gnawing at him.

When he woke, he saw that the shadows across the woods and fields had grown longer. Cole didn't need a watch to tell him it was six o'clock, then seven. When it was dark enough, he crept out from behind the rock and limped toward the road, feeling like a beaten dog.

Vaccaro emerged from the shadows of the hedgerow, where he'd been sitting, rifle across his knees. The squad that they'd rescued had long since moved on.

"Cole, is that you?" Vaccaro asked, alarm plain in the city boy's voice. "Why the hell did you shoot at me?"

"I was tryin' to keep your fool head from gettin' blowed off."

"What the hell happened out there? You said this was supposed to be like a game of hounds and fox."

"Turns out that there was more than one fox," Cole said.

He meant to take another step toward Vaccaro, but found that it turned into a stagger.

Vaccaro caught him, and for the first time noticed the blood soaking Cole's uniform. "You dumbass hillbilly, you went and got yourself shot!"

CHAPTER THIRTEEN

COLE LIMPED into the French chateau that served as a forward command post, trailing blood. He looked like hell, and felt about the same. He had scratches on his face from diving for cover in the field. Blood covered his uniform. He took off his helmet that was decorated with the Confederate flag, revealing hair that was matted to his head with sweat. He could smell himself.

Vaccaro lurched in behind him, not looking much better. He was more than a little shaken that some German sniper had gotten the better of Cole.

It was full dark by now. The fighting had knocked out any electricity, so the command post was lighted by a few candles that wavered in the evening breeze. A kerosene lantern was smoking up the interior. Only vestiges of the chateau's grandeur remained, such as the high ceilings and finely carved woodwork. The Germans had looted most everything of value, leaving behind echoing rooms, cracked walls, and peeling paint. The dim, flickering light emphasized Cole's battered and hollow-eyed countenance.

Lieutenant Mulholland saw them and hurried over.

"What the hell happened to you guys?" the lieutenant asked, looking alarmed.

"We got shot at."

Mulholland grabbed for Cole's arm, turned him toward what light there was, and winced at the sight of the bloody furrow cut by the enemy sniper's bullet. "Dammit, Cole. You of all people are not supposed to get shot. If the Germans can shoot you, then they can shoot anybody."

"I hate to break this to you, sir, but I sure as hell ain't bulletproof." Cole sank to the stone floor along one wall. He noticed that the room was so big that the cabin in Gashey's Creek would fit inside.

The lieutenant hovered over him like a mother hen. He decided that maybe he had been wrong about Mulholland wanting to get rid of him. Some officers had gathered in a corner and were waving at Mulholland, so he gave Cole a pat on his good shoulder and promised to be back.

Vaccaro grabbed a canteen from a nearby soldier. Cole tilted it up and guzzled water, the muscles of his throat working under the surface like pistons. He drank until the canteen ran dry.

"Let me see that shoulder," Vaccaro said. He bent down and unbuttoned Cole's jacket and shirt, then eased it off. The fabric was stiff with dried blood. He got a rag, wet it, and dabbed at Cole's wound to get a look at the damage. He whistled.

"Bet that hurts like hell," he said.

"I've seen worse," Cole said. He craned his neck to inspect the wound, wincing at the sight of the raw flesh.

"You know what? Another couple of inches to the right and your head would be missing."

"You got a real bedside manner, City Boy."

"Let me get the medic over here to fix you up."

"I don't need a goddamn medic. I need a drink."

"Looks to me like you could use both."

Vaccaro left in search of a medic and some alcohol, leaving Cole sitting there alone. Now that he was back in the relative safety of the command post, a thousand thoughts swirled through his mind, not the least of which was that he was lucky to be alive. You didn't almost get killed without dwelling on that.

Sure, he'd only been grazed across the shoulder. That wouldn't even get him a Purple Heart—as if he gave a damn about such things. But it hurt like hell. Most important of all, the German sniper had gotten a piece of him. That shoulder hadn't been much of a target. Cole guessed that the target he had presented wasn't any bigger than a playing card, and yet the German had managed to hit him from that barn.

The German sniper was that good, and it was unnerving.

He had already dealt with one nasty German sniper named Von Stenger. They'd had a showdown in a flooded field outside the little French crossroads town of Bienville. That was the same encounter in which Jolie Molyneaux had been shot.

He did not know whether or not Von Stenger had survived their final encounter. It seemed unlikely, but Cole couldn't be one hundred percent sure. If Von Stenger still lived, it wasn't from lack of effort on Cole's part.

But something about today's encounter had him thinking that it wasn't Von Stenger that he had run across. Snipers had a style, and this one's style was different. He and Von Stenger had a history, and Cole was certain that the German wouldn't have let him crawl out of there alive. He would have made sure to finish the job, one way or another. Von Stenger knew better than to let Cole live to fight another day.

The only conclusion Cole could reach was that this must be a different sniper. Just as deadly, and just as much of a marksman as his old adversary.

He shook his head, feeling like a kicked dog. What was it with these Germans? What made them so ruthless? Give them a rifle with a telescopic sight, and they were all a bunch of goddamn killers.

Cole reached for the full canteen that Vaccaro had left behind and found that his hand was shaking. He had been through D-Day and then the fight at Bienville without getting the shakes. He wrapped both hands around the canteen in order to lift it to his lips.

Vaccaro returned with the medic, who was instantly recognizable by the red cross in a white circle on his helmet and the white armband with its red cross on his left arm.

"Let's have a look," the medic said. The poor guy looked exhausted, as if he might fall asleep on his feet.

"It ain't nothin'," Cole said. "Jest a scratch."

"Some scratch," the medic said, then set about cleaning and binding the wound. He coated it heavily with sulfa powder. He was so intent on Cole's wound that he only noticed the rifle with its telescopic sight propped against the wall as he finished up. "Sniper, huh?" Then he studied Cole's face more intently. "Hey, you're the guy I read about."

"If you say so," Cole said noncommittally.

Vaccaro spoke up. "Yeah, he's the one. Got a story written about him by none other than Ernie Pyle. How's that for famous?"

"I'd ask for your autograph if I had a pen." To Cole's surprise, the medic seemed to mean it. "Shoot a Kraut for me, will ya?"

Cole said nothing.

"You've lost some blood, so be sure to drink lots of water and make sure you get something to eat. Sugar would be good for starters. You'll need to keep that dressing dry, and stay off your feet for a few days if possible."

"I appreciate the thought, pardner," Cole said. "But in case you ain't noticed, there's a war on."

"I hear you," the medic said. "But it's my job to say it, right? You know, in the German army, if you suffer a flesh wound or get shot through the meat of your leg, you get five days to recuperate. That's the rule in the Wehrmacht. Then, it's back to the front."

"Does this look like the German army to you?"

"What I'm sayin' is, the Krauts have their backs against the wall and they still give their soldiers five days to recover." He nodded at the bandaged shoulder. "If that wound of yours festers, you'll be out of commission for a lot longer."

"Like I said, thanks for the advice."

The medic finished and moved off to help the next man; there was no shortage of patients.

Vaccaro had managed to find Cole a fresh shirt—one that was only slightly used—and helped him put it on. For now, Cole would have to make do with his bloody jacket.

"What do you think that medic meant with all that talk about wounded Germans?" Cole asked. "Whose side is he on?"

"Don't get your shorts in a twist, Hillbilly. He was just trying to help."

"You didn't have to tell him about the newspaper article."

"Hey, he recognized you from the photo. See, you're getting to be famous. I saved you a copy of that newspaper story, by the way," Vaccaro said. "I can't believe you didn't want to read it."

"Why in hell would I want to read about myself?"

"Here, take my copy. It will give you something to do while you recuperate." Vaccaro reached into his pocket and took out a scrap of newspaper, carefully folded and wrapped in plastic to keep it protected from the mud and rain.

Cole shook his head. "I'm too tired to fool with that right now."

"Go on, take it."

"Do I look like I've got time to read?"

"Suit yourself." Vaccaro put the paper away. He reached into another pocket and this time pulled out a flask. "I know he put some sulfa powder on that arm, but this will help cure you on the inside."

"What is this stuff?"

"Calvados." Vaccaro grinned and waggled his eyebrows. "Otherwise known as French moonshine. That ought to make you feel right at home."

"Moonshine my ass." Still, Cole took a swig. And another. The apple brandy that was a specialty of Normandy went down a lot easier than any moonshine Cole had tasted. He drank deeply again.

"Careful now, Hillbilly. Between the booze and that flesh wound there, some officer might court martial you under Article 92."

"Yeah? What's that?" If there was one thing that Cole knew about the Army, it was that it never tired of rules and regulations. The Army had more rules than a witch had warts.

"Cole, how do you get through this world being such an ignorant hillbilly?" Vaccaro reached for the flask, took a pull, gave it back. "Article 92 concerns dereliction of duty by rendering oneself unfit by self-inflicted wounds or drunkenness."

"Shee-it. Article 92? You sound like a lawyer." Cole drank. He had not eaten much, and he could feel the liquor go right to his head. "Like to see 'em try to pin that on me."

After another couple of drinks, he attempted to get to his feet. His shoulder felt sore as hell but he didn't need it to walk, and he didn't need his left shoulder to shoot. In other words, there wasn't going to be any dereliction of duty.

He took two shuffling steps like an old man, ignoring the pain. He stumbled, knocking painfully against a pile of wooden crates that someone had brought in to fuel the fireplace. Angrily, he grabbed one of the crates using his good arm and smashed it to the ground. It felt so good to smash something that he grabbed another crate and turned it into kindling.

Nearby, an officer looked up in irritation. "Knock it off, soldier."

Cole thought about bashing the next crate over the officer's head, and he might have, if he hadn't felt a hand on his arm.

"Easy there, Cole," Vaccaro said. "Let's get some chow, and then maybe some sleep."

Cole shrugged off Vaccaro's hand. The motion made him wince. "I'm fine, goddammit."

"You'll feel better once you eat. Remember what that medic said."

Mostly, they had subsisted on K rations for the last few days. But the cooks had gone to work in the chateau's old kitchen, which was like something out of the last century, complete with soapstone counters and a stone sink. There was hot coffee, and spaghetti. It smelled delicious, and Vaccaro got plates for them both. Cole's hand shook as he took the plate.

Vaccaro couldn't help but notice. "What's gotten into you?"

"Nothin'," Cole responded.

The look that Vaccaro gave him indicated that he didn't believe it for a minute.

Normally, Vaccaro thought, Cole was cool as ice. Nothing much rattled his cage. Now, he was smashing things and trying to eat with shaking hands. What the hell was wrong with him? That German sniper had really gotten to him.

Vaccaro was wise enough to leave Cole alone. The two men ate in silence. When they were finished, Vaccaro said, "Get some sleep, Hillbilly. You'll feel better in the morning. I'll talk to the lieutenant. Maybe he can get you sent to the rear for a day or two."

"Like hell," Cole said. "In the morning, I am going after that Kraut son of a bitch who shot me."

Vaccaro looked at him incredulously. "Hillbilly, we just got our asses kicked by that German. Don't be in any hurry to find him again."

"Don't worry, City Boy. That German ain't gonna be so lucky the second time around."

Cole had spoken with more bravado than he felt. The truth was that some feelings you didn't shake—like getting shot. Vaccaro was right. That German had damn near killed him, and would've killed Vaccaro too. It had been a while since Cole had encountered anyone that good. They were lucky to be alive.

Since coming ashore on D-Day, Cole had grappled with a whole whirlwind of emotions, from fear to anger to loss. He had seen too many good men die.

But now he felt a gnawing doubt. Somewhere out there was a German sniper who had almost killed him today. Cole felt like he'd been lucky. What if they met again? What about the next German sniper? Had Cole just been lucky all this time in France? Luck eventually burned out, like a candle.

The question was, had Cole's luck truly run out, or had he simply met his match today?

He was half drunk now, and dizzy with exhaustion. On the way to the door, he shoved a soldier out of the way. The man rounded on him angrily, saw the expression on Cole's face, and walked away. Cole had shoved a man, but it felt like he was shoving the thoughts out of his mind.

Cole was a survivor. He had grown up in a mountain shack

without electricity or running water. He had known cold and hunger. Yet he had endured.

He thought of his pa, who had every trait in common with a rattlesnake when he'd been drinking corn liquor. When he was sober, pa had taught him what it meant to survive in the mountains. His knowledge was considerable. If he'd been born a hundred years earlier, pa would have been a real mountain man like the Coles who had come before. Instead, he had mostly been a moonshiner, but pa had known more about the woods and mountains than anyone alive.

Pa had always said that when you were cold, when there were miles to go, when maybe there was something tracking *you* instead of the other way around, well, you could whine and be afraid all you wanted. Being afraid didn't do a bit of good. The mountain sure as hell didn't give a damn.

"You got to get your dander up, boy. You want to live, you got to fight."

Cole thought about that now.

"I'll get that son of a bitch and nail his Nazi hide to the barn door."

Vaccaro snorted. "Look at you, Cole. You're a mess. You can hardly walk, and you want to go after the Kraut who did this to you? You are one crazy son of a bitch."

Cole couldn't argue with that. He spread some blankets on the ground and tried to sleep, but every time he closed his eyes, he relived that moment of getting hit. Finally, he just lay awake, thinking of the mountains back home.

CHAPTER FOURTEEN

"AH, THERE YOU ARE, ROHDE."

"Yes, sir."

Captain Fischer had sent for him, which was worrisome. He suspected that Fischer would either want to scold him for some perceived infraction or send him on some hare-brained mission.

He felt tired after hunkering in the barn most of the day before, and while he had certainly winged the American sniper who had, by good fortune, ended up in Rohde's sights, he had not killed him outright as he had hoped. Of course, without corroboration, there would have been no credit for killing the American sniper.

Rohde had already made his report, and was thinking about working a different sector today. Considering that the countryside was crawling with Allied troops, there was no shortage of targets.

When he entered the command post, he was surprised to find that Fischer was not alone. With him was a Waffen SS officer whom Rohde did not recognize, a man who was rather short and rotund to be an SS officer. He was also old enough to be Rohde's father, or even Fischer's father, for that matter. This was no battle squad leader, yet he managed to project an air of self-satisfied competence, not unlike a Zurich banker.

Normally, Rohde was casual with Fischer, but in the presence of the SS officer he came to attention and saluted smartly.

"At ease, Rohde. This is Major Dorfmann from the Skorpion unit," Fischer explained. "He is the man responsible for the *Luftpost*."

Rohde was familiar with the *Luftpost*; it was the equivalent of the weekly newspaper for soldiers at the front.

Rohde eyed both officers with apprehension. The major might be a journalist, but an SS officer was an SS officer. Rohde shifted uncomfortably from foot to foot, wondering what Fischer and Dorfmann wanted with him. He decided that he would find out soon enough.

While he appreciated the fact that Captain Fischer had taken him under his wing and encouraged him as a sniper, Rohde well understood that Fischer was, in part, motivated by self-interest. Whatever his star sniper accomplished also reflected well on the captain. Rohde had the uncomfortable feeling of being something of a status symbol, like a fine racehorse or hunting dog.

Fischer had not come up through the rank and file, but had essentially been born into the officer's corp. He was from a wealthy family that was more than likely quite used to owning a stable of fine horses and hunting dogs. Yet what happened to a horse that was no longer useful? The lucky ones got put out to pasture. More often than not, they were trundled off to the slaughterhouse for whatever value could be gotten from their hides, hooves, and meat. Aristocrats such as Fischer were not much given to sentiment where profit was involved. Rohde was sure that he would be favored only as long as he was useful.

"Yesterday, you said that you encountered an American sniper. One with some insignia painted on his helmet," Fischer said.

"Yes, sir. That would be correct."

Rohde was on his guard. He had only mentioned the insignia in passing, yet the captain seemed to be making a big deal out of it. He wondered where this was going, and why the captain cared so much about one enemy soldier. Normally, the captain was only interested in numbers. How many Rohde had shot, not who. The battlefield was nothing if not anonymous. What could be so special about one man? Rohde guessed that he was about to find out.

The captain turned to the SS officer. "Major?"

The SS officer stepped forward. In his hand was a newspaper, but not the familiar *Luftpost*. The newspaper was folded to isolate a headline and article, which, to Rohde's surprise, was written in English. He recognized the language, although he couldn't speak a word of it. There was also a photograph accompanying the article. With a nod, the SS officer invited him to take a closer look. What Rohde saw was a grainy black and white photograph on newsprint, but it was detailed enough. The photograph revealed a lean, fox-like face under the American helmet, on the front of which was painted the same insignia he had seen on the sniper's helmet yesterday.

"Does that soldier look familiar?" the officer asked.

"I don't know that I would recognize the face, sir," Rohde said carefully. "However, his helmet had the same insignia."

The captain and major exchanged a knowing glance.

"It is not unit insignia," the captain said, turning back to his sniper. "At least, not from this war! It is a flag. I would not expect you to know American history, Rohde, so let me enlighten you. This is what is known as a Confederate flag, the symbol of rebellious forces during the American Civil War. Some Americans from the South still favor this symbol, known as 'the Stars and Bars,' as a nod to their heritage."

"Yes, sir," Rohde said when the captain looked at him expectantly. Rohde still had no clue what this was about.

"The sniper in the newspaper article has such a flag painted on his helmet," the SS major added helpfully. "This is the sniper that you shot yesterday."

"I wounded him, sir. That is correct."

Rohde peered intently at the article, but could puzzle out nothing else. His English was marginal at best. Like most German soldiers, he could understand and speak a smattering of English words. The spoken languages were similar in some ways. Reading anything written in English was another matter.

The SS major saw him looking. "Do you know English, Rohde?"

"No sir."

"No matter," the SS major said in a dismissive tone that made Rohde dislike him immediately. "I will summarize it for you. This sniper is called Micajah Cole, and he is from the Appalachian Mountains. These are much like our own Hartz Mountains. He is what the Americans call a hillbilly. He was quite the hunter growing up, according to the article."

"What does this have to do with me, sir?"

"I am getting there, Rohde! Let me finish. This article was written by a famous American journalist named Ernie Pyle. He likes to go among the troops and write about their strug-gles to encourage the people back home. You might call him something of a pastoralist, like Goethe. His epic poem *Hermann and Dorothea* comes to mind."

Here the major paused and looked at Fischer, as if Rohde would have no idea what he was talking about. Truth be told, he did not know the poem. One could not be German and not have heard of Goethe, but that was the limit of Rohde's knowledge. The smug officer had a pale, fat forehead and Rohde could not resist imagining the satisfaction it would give him to put a bullet hole in the center of it.

"Ah, Goethe," Fischer said, putting a vague but fond look on his face. The SS major seemed satisfied with Fischer's show of literary appreciation, but Rohde was not convinced. The only thing that Rohde had ever seen the captain read intently were pornographic French magazines.

Rohde was not as dim as the major seemed to think. He could see where this was going. "That is the sniper I wounded. I shot their hero."

The major's face lit up. "You did, indeed. Well done, Rohde! It is my role to exploit opportunities such as this. You see, we publish a newspaper in English that is dropped by the Luftwaffe over the American forces, in order to share our viewpoint with them. We even put it in artillery shells for special delivery, ha, ha, so that copies are scattered behind enemy lines. We call it *Lightning News: Condensed News for Service Men*. Nothing over the top, you know, but enough to plant a seed of doubt in their minds. Subtle but effective, you see. It has been a very successful campaign."

The major showed him a copy of a newspaper with a front-page photograph that showed an American GI kissing a girl, with the famous Big Ben clock tower in the background. The prettiness of the girl got Rohde's attention. "This was our most recent issue. Very popular! I've been told that some of the English troops we captured last week were carrying copies, ha, ha! The article here is about Americans in England stealing all the local girls while the English boys are off doing the fighting."

"Is it true?" Rohde blurted out.

The very idea of GIs stealing the local girls made him indignant, even if he wasn't English.

The major laughed, clearly pleased with himself. "See, that is exactly the result I am going for! The English troops will now be jealous of the Americans and mistrust them. Two weeks ago, the front page article was about blacks and Jews making love to all the lonely girls back home in America. The article simply nurtures what some GIs already suspected, you see. Where there is a seed of doubt, we water it. We confirm their nagging fears. My next issue is going to be about you shooting their heroic sniper."

The major invited him to sit, and for the next thirty minutes he peppered Rohde with questions about everything from his boyhood upbringing to his tactics. Rohde answered carefully, not wanting to seem anything less than a loyal German. The major seemed a little disappointed that Rohde did not have a sweetheart back home.

"No one writes you letters? What is wrong with our young girls?" he demanded, then sighed. "They are not doing their part. Not to worry, I will give you a nice girl back home named Heidi, or maybe Greta."

Rohde did not tell him about the French girl, of course.

When the interview ended, the major called in a photographer. He had Rohde pose with his rifle, and also with an American combat helmet on which was painted a Confederate flag.

"How did you get this from him?" Rohde asked in wonder.

"Do you think that this is actually the American's helmet? Wonderful! Keep thinking that! There, hold it up like a trophy!"

The camera flash popped again and again, until Rohde's eyes danced with spots.

When the photo session was finished, the major gathered his notes and patted Rohde on the shoulder. "Don't worry, Rohde. You are going to be famous!"

"Sir, will this be in the *Luftpost* and the *Völkischer Beobachter*?" Rohde asked. The second newspaper was the official publication of the Nazi party, distributed nationwide.

"We will start by informing the enemy so that they fear you," Major Dorfmann said. "This story will be distributed to the Allies in my *Lightning News*. That is the priority."

"May I add something to the interview, Herr Major?"

The major seemed puzzled at first, but then flipped to a blank page in his notebook and looked indulgently at Rohde. "Of course."

"You did not ask me why I want to be the best sniper possible."

"Maybe you should be the journalist, ha, ha," the major said. "But I think I know your answer. Why, you wish to serve the Fatherland, of course! And to make your parents proud."

Rohde stiffened. "My parents are already proud of both their sons."

The major looked knowingly at Fischer, and then back at Rohde. It was clear that he knew all about Rohde's older brother. Had Fischer told him, or did the whole goddamn SS know? "This article is for the Allies. They know nothing about your brother. Besides, your brother may have deserted, but you are a hero for the Fatherland."

"My brother was not a deserter," Rohde said coldly.

The SS major blinked, at a loss for words for the first time. Captain Fischer spoke up, breaking the uncomfortable silence. He sounded annoyed that his star sniper had been impertinent with the SS major. "The major here is writing about *you*, Rohde, not your brother. Come now, have some sense. You are doing this for the Fatherland and your parents, and leave it at that."

"And for one more thing, sir," Rohde said.

"What's that?" the major asked, his perpetual smile growing thin.

"I want to win the Iron Cross."

Relieved, the major grinned widely at that answer. "That's the spirit, Rohde! Ha, ha! Kill this American sniper and I shall put a story about you on the front page of *Völkischer Beobachter* that will be read in Berlin by the leader himself!"

CHAPTER FIFTEEN

TO HIS SURPRISE, Rohde found that in the wake of the interview with the SS major that he was more excited than he might have expected. It was not the prospect of being on the front page of a newspaper going out to enemy troops that enthused him so much as the thought of being noticed by one enemy soldier in particular—the sniper that he had wounded in the field.

Given the vagaries of the battlefield, they might never meet again. Major Dorfmann's newspaper would pour salt in the enemy sniper's wound and doubt upon his soul.

He had seen that sniper shoot, and the American was very good. If they ever did encounter one another in the field, Rohde was certain that he would now have the mental edge over the American.

The SS major had said that the American journalist Ernie Pyle had made this Cole into a hero. Now, he would be a tarnished hero, having been bested by a German sniper. With a single bullet, Rohde had shown him what was what and given him a taste of German superiority. Rohde had definitively answered the question of who was the better man.

Most of all, the article left him excited by the prospect of being noticed by someone other than Captain Fischer. The article was not the Iron Cross, but it was an affirmation of Rohde's talents. His coveted medal might very well follow.

What if he did get put into the Berlin news and the paper crossed the desk of none other than Hitler himself? It was a daydream, of course, but it could clinch the Iron Cross for him.

How he ached for that bit of metal. The other soldiers sometimes joked about an Iron Cross being worth no more than a few pfennig. And yet, it was so much more than a piece of cheap tin. In Rohde's mind, the Iron Cross represented respect and redemption. He did not doubt his older brother, but others did. Winning the Iron Cross would put those doubts to rest for once and for all. The Iron Cross was not just for Dieter or for Carl; the medal would be for them both.

Carl had been six years older. The family had lived just outside Mannheim—so far, the family home had been spared destruction by Allied air raids. His father worked in one of the factories that the British bombers were so intent on destroying. Many of the small city's beautiful old buildings were now ruined or damaged, including the Mannheim Palace that had once been home to German aristocrats and whose grand architecture had been the pride of the city. He could not quote poetry, but he knew what Goethe had said about architecture being frozen music. He remembered how he and Carl had both been awed by the palace as boys; it was likely a ruin now, another vestige of childhood.

Dieter thought back to those years before the war. If he and Carl had been closer in age, there might have been more competition, more of a sibling rivalry, and thus different feelings toward his brother. But a difference in age of six years between two boys is vast. It meant that Carl was always the bigger and stronger one. The one that Dieter could look up to. And Carl looked out for him. He had even shown Dieter how to shave.

Once, an older boy had gotten it into his head to pick on Dieter, as boys will do. There was no real rhyme or reason for it. It started with some name-calling and shoving in the schoolyard. Dieter was no coward, but when he squared off against the bigger boy, whose name was Lenerz, Dieter did not have a chance. The older boy must have outweighed him by forty pounds and was a good fifteen centimeters taller. Dieter went home that day with a fat lip and a black eye, but it was mostly his pride that was wounded.

"Who did this to you?" Carl wanted to know.

"Never mind," Dieter said. The last thing he wanted to be was a tattletale, especially to his brother. He could fight his own battles. "It doesn't matter."

"Was it that fat bastard Lenerz?"

Dieter just shrugged.

"I thought so. He is my age! He ought to know better than to go around picking on you—or anybody else, for that matter."

That was all that Carl said about it. But the next day at school, it was Lenerz who had a fat lip and a black eye. He never again so much as looked in Dieter's direction.

It was simply Carl's nature to stick up for others. He was indignant on behalf of the underdog, whether it was his little brother or a war-torn nation. Germany had seen itself as the underdog, and so naturally, Carl had come to its defense, like so many other young men.

The only time that Dieter had been jealous of Carl was when his brother had first come home in his SS uniform. Dieter ached to be a soldier, but he was much too young.

Then the war began. Everyone could remember that day in 1939 when the news came that German troops had invaded

Poland. Then France fell. The English army was nearly driven into the sea at Dunkirk. Those were heady and glorious days when anything seemed possible, when Germany was on the march, and any young man who could was eager to rush into uniform.

When word arrived that Carl was dead, it was delivered in a terse telegram from the SS. A single sentence stated that Carl Rohde had been shot for desertion.

Neither his father nor his mother, and especially not Dieter, had believed a word of it. They had their theories. Carl must have been visiting a girl—he had been handsome enough—or some other adventure had taken him away from his unit. Perhaps he had defied orders by being drawn into the defense of another underdog, to his detriment. There were rumors about darker things being done by the SS, and Carl may not have felt that he had signed on for that.

It was likely that they would never know the truth of what happened, not when the SS was involved. But could Carl have been a coward? Had he deserted his duty? Never. Never in a thousand years.

In unguarded moments, Dieter sometimes wondered how it must have been for Carl in his final moments, waiting to be shot. His last thoughts would have been of home and family. Then the clap of a gunshot, a flash of white light, and eternal nothingness. Death was like the time before one was born, a return to nonexistence. Imagining Carl's last moments pushed Rohde toward despair, so he did his best not to think about it.

While there had never been any official announcement about Carl's fate, rumors had gotten around back home. There were whispers. Some of their neighbors looked at Dieter and his parents with disgust, but what was even worse was the fact that far more looked at them with pity, especially the ones who had sons and husbands in the military. They knew very well that any one of them might be the next to receive such a telegram. Dieter hated those pitying looks worst of all.

And now, here was his chance at redemption by being a sniper who won the Iron Cross, not just for himself, but for his mother and father. And most of all, in some small way, it would mean redemption for Carl.

CHAPTER SIXTEEN

"Look at this shit," Vaccaro said, holding up a copy of a newspaper. The paper was new and smelled strongly of fresh ink, unlike the stale newspapers that made it to the front. They were bivouacked not far from the command post, relaxing in the shade cast by a stone wall. "This is that *Lightning News* we keep finding around. I know the Krauts must write it, but at least it's something to read. It doesn't make bad ass wipe, either."

"You know I don't waste my time on them newspapers," Cole said.

Cole was busy cleaning his rifle, and Vaccaro stopped talking long enough to watch. Vaccaro was convinced that Cole had the cleanest rifle in the Army. His own weapon was fortunate to get wiped down with an oily rag just in time to keep the rust at bay. The lessons of basic training had not stuck with him.

In contrast, Cole polished the bolt action and chamber so lovingly that it was almost like he was stroking a lover. Cole was the kind of person who focused on a task and blocked out everything else. In fact, if it hadn't been for that business with Jolie Molyneaux, Vaccaro might have thought that Cole was more interested in guns than women.

"So you don't read newspapers, huh? What happens when you need to know something?"

"I know plenty," Cole said. "If there's any news I missed, then I reckon you'll tell me whether I want to hear it or not."

"Well, you ought to take a look at this."

"City Boy, I done told you—"

Before Cole could protest further, Vaccaro thrust the newspaper at him. "Recognize anything?"

Left without much choice due to the newspaper interposed between himself and the rifle, Cole looked. As usual, the words made as much sense to him as bird tracks across the page.

He still hadn't told Vaccaro that he could not read. Not for the first time, he regretted never having ventured into the one-room schoolhouse that was only a five-mile walk from the family cabin at Gashey's Creek. His pa never had made him go, saying that a body would spend his time better in the woods or doin' chores instead of book learnin'. Pa always pronounced those last two words with a disgusted snarl. *Book learnin'.*

Pa had been perversely proud of not being able to read. His mother could puzzle out a few words, but she struggled too much with reading to teach her children. Cole had once shared his father's pride in having no use for learning his letters, but the war had made him see that a man needed reading and writing to take his place in the world. He now hid his illiteracy even from Vaccaro.

As it turned out, Cole did not need to read to understand the front page photograph of a baby-faced German soldier, dressed in a sniper's camouflage uniform and holding a scoped rifle in one hand. Tucked under the German soldier's other arm was a GI helmet with a Confederate flag painted on it.

"I'll be damned," Cole said. He touched the helmet on his head that was decorated with a similar flag. His had been painted by Jimmy Turner, the gentle mountain boy who had died minutes after coming ashore at Omaha Beach on D Day. "I thought mine was the only one."

Vaccaro snatched back the newspaper and said harshly, "It's supposed to be *your* helmet, you dumb hillbilly. Didn't you at least read the picture caption?"

Cole glared at Vaccaro. His eyes were silvery as the water in a mountain river and as empty of emotion as the feral gaze of a wolf. Unconsciously, Vaccaro recoiled from that gaze.

The last time Vaccaro had seen eyes like that, they had belonged to a contract killer for the Irish mob. There was no shortage of mobsters in Brooklyn, but generally speaking, the Irish and Italians didn't mix. It was downright unhealthy for anyone Irish to be caught in the Italian neighborhood where Vaccaro lived, especially after dark. The hitman had a girlfriend there that he liked to visit, but everyone left him alone.

Vaccaro lightened his tone. "That's a picture of the German who shot you. Lieutenant Mulholland says the German's name is pronounced *Row-duh*. He's some hotshot sniper, apparently, who's been racking up the kills."

"Well, he damn near got me. I'll give him that much."

"That's what the article says. Hell, the article even has your *name*. They must have picked it up from that piece Ernie Pyle wrote about you. You're getting to be famous, Cole. The German must have seen your helmet and put two and two together."

"But that ain't *my* helmet he's holdin'."

"Cole, I hate to break this to you, but the Krauts invented jet engines and rockets and nerve gas. Don't you think they could figure out how to paint a Johnny Reb flag on a helmet and take a picture of it? It's a little thing called propaganda."

"Maybe they done that," Cole agreed. He paused. "What else does it say?"

Vaccaro offered the newspaper. "Christ on a cross, Cole. Do I look like your personal secretary? You can read it for yourself."

Cole studied the face in the photograph more closely. So this was the German who had shot him? The German looked more like a schoolboy than a sniper. Nonetheless, Cole felt a chill run through him. He was in no hurry to run into that kid again.

Cole waved Vaccaro off with the cleaning rag. "Can't you see I'm busy? Just tell me if it says anything important."

For once, Vaccaro clammed up. Cole prompted him, "Well?"

"It says that this German sniper is gonna finish you off."

Cole said nothing, but only continued to clean his rifle. From the sounds of things, he would be needing it again soon and he would need every advantage that he could get.

ROHDE DECIDED that he liked his chances as a sniper better if he had a different rifle. He was convinced that the bolt action K98 had cost him his killing shot against the American sniper. It simply took too much time to chamber another round. The bolt had that annoying tendency to stick, and when he whacked it into place with the heel of his hand it cost him precious time.

He had a solution for that. The Gewehr Model 43 rifle.

The trouble was, that bald bastard Hohenfeldt who ran the armory just laughed when Rohde asked about upgrading his rifle. Hohenfeldt oversaw the distribution of small arms and ammunition as if each rifle belonged to him personally.

He went to see Fischer about it.

"I would have gotten that American sniper if I hadn't been shooting that damn old rifle of mine," Rohde said, hastily adding, "Sir."

"There is nothing wrong with your rifle, Rohde."

"Hohenfeldt has one of the new Gewehr Model 43s just sitting there in the armory. If I'd had that, I wouldn't have missed."

The captain shook his head. "Your equipment is fine."

"The Gewehr is a semi-automatic. With a weapon like that, there is no need to take one's eye away from the sight between shots to work the action."

"I am aware of how a rifle works, Rohde," the captain said testily, taking umbrage to the sniper's tone.

"But sir, he has one just sitting there!"

"Look here, Rohde. I am not going to get involved in how Hohenfeldt runs the armory. Our Staber knows his business. If he won't issue that new rifle to you, he must have his reasons."

Right, Rohde was thinking. *It's because I don't have a bowl of fat sausages to trade for it.*

Rohde was not all that surprised by Fischer's reluctance to get involved. It was no secret that most officers would not interfere with how a seasoned noncommissioned officer ran a supply operation. What he said was, "Yes, sir."

Rodhe knew better than to push too hard with the captain, who had already given him an enormous amount of leeway. Fischer was nothing if not mercurial. He would tolerate Rohde so long as he was useful and not too demanding. Once he became a pain in the Hauptmann's ass, that was it. But Rohde wanted that rifle, so he would just have to come up with a way of obtaining it.

If there was one quality that Rohde possessed—in addition to being a good shot—it was determination.

Fischer said, "Never mind the rifle. At the rate you are going, you are going to be famous, Rohde!"

"Yes, sir."

"If you get killed, the SS will just make up a sniper who sounds even better than you are, ha, ha! I suspect that Major Dorfmann could turn a turnip into a roast beef if need be. In any case, if Dorfmann gets you into the Berlin newspapers it should make your family proud and make up for this bad business about your brother."

"Sir?"

I don't hold your brother's actions against you, Rohde. No one does. Some men are not up to the task and disgrace themselves—and their families."

Rohde's face burned. He knew very well that his brother was not a coward. Just in time, he bit back the angry retort on his lips, knowing that he could only go so far with Fischer.

"There is one thing that will set it right, sir."

"What's that, Rohde?"

"Just what I told the major. Winning that Iron Cross, sir. I was not joking when I said that to Major Dorfmann. You are the one who would have to put my name in for it when the time comes." He hastily added again, "Sir."

Fischer remained silent, staring at him nonplussed. Rohde worried that he had overstepped his bounds. Nobody asked his commanding officer for a medal. But the German military was not one to frown upon ambition. There was no higher ambition than to earn the Iron Cross.

Much to his relief, the captain laughed. He clapped Rohde

on the shoulder. "You have style, Rohde! I saw that in you, which is why I made you a sniper. It is a shame that you did not finish off that American sniper. Maybe next time. Meanwhile, keep shooting Amis like you have been doing, and you will win that Iron Cross yet!"

CHAPTER SEVENTEEN

"MAIL CALL!"

At the shout from the mail orderly, a group of GIs pressed around. It was something of a logistical miracle that personal mail got through to the front lines, never mind the fact that the letters and packages from home were sometimes weeks getting there. The mail was certainly a morale builder, but more than that, it was a matter of pride that the mail got through. The military postal service was not going to let a thousand miles of ocean, scores of U-boats, and a hostile Wehrmacht stop the mail.

Vaccaro pushed his way to the front of the group. He almost always got a package from home, or at least a letter. The package contents were invariably practical and sometimes delicious. Socks, one week. Homemade Italian cookies and candy, another week. Once, an entire cake had arrived. That had made Vaccaro the most popular guy in the squad.

Vaccaro was still waiting for his latest package when Cole's name was called.

Cole never got mail. The mail orderly paused and glanced

at the label a second time before stating more quizzically, "Cole?"

"I'll take that." Vaccaro grabbed the package and waded to the back of the crowd, where Cole was going over his rifle with an oily rag. He thrust the neatly wrapped box at him, giving it a good shake in the process to try and hear what was inside. No luck there. "Hell must be freezing over, Hillbilly. You got a package."

"Must be cookies," Cole said nonchalantly. He kept on cleaning his rifle.

"You can't tell me that somebody back home in Possum Holler or wherever you're from made you a batch of cookies. Maybe it's moonshine."

"Blow it out your ass, Vaccaro," Cole said, reaching for the box, not quite successfully hiding a grin. He was just as curious as Vaccaro as to the contents of the package. "Give that here."

"Is it from your mama?"

Cole glanced at the return address. He couldn't actually read, but he could recognize names. "No, it ain't from my mama. Not unless she done changed her name to Hollis Bailey."

"Who the hell is that?"

"An old friend from back home."

The cardboard box within was neatly wrapped in heavy brown paper tied with the sort of rough twine that gardeners favored. Judging from the label on the box, it had once held canning jars. Maybe Vaccaro wasn't that far off about the moonshine.

Hollis had not bothered with a note. A narrow object lay inside, carefully wrapped in layer after layer of newspaper.

"Is there anything in there or is that just a box full of old newspapers?" Vaccaro asked.

"Hollis always liked to say that if you think one nail is good enough, then better make it two."

"Ah, the wisdom of Possum Holler. You ought to write a book."

By now, a little crowd had gathered thanks to Vaccaro's loud mouth. Cole was something of a man of mystery to the rest of the company. He kept to himself. He definitely never talked about home or sweethearts. He never received so much as a postcard.

The thought of someone like Cole getting cookies in the mail seemed ridiculous. It was as if he had arrived fully formed as a sniper, hands forever wrapped around a scoped rifle and clear-cut eyes scanning the horizon. Vaccaro had joked about moonshine, which seemed more likely.

If Cole had, in fact, gotten a jar of moonshine, they all wanted a taste.

Cole unwrapped the object that had been so carefully sent these many miles and held it up. The final layer of wrapping was a Confederate flag about a foot long, just the size that bystanders might wave at a parade. Just the size to mark a grave.

Cole stretched out the flag and admired it.

Vaccaro was busy looking over Cole's shoulder at the contents of the box. "I'll be damned," he said, more than a little awestruck by what he saw.

* * *

THE COLE FAMILY and Hollis Bailey went back a ways. Hollis lived two miles as the crow flies from the Cole family shack on Gashey's Creek. In the mountains, it helped to be a crow or to have two good feet if you wanted to get somewhere. The Coles were so far back in the woods that nothing more than a trail led to their place. Nobody was driving a car back in there, that was for damn sure. It was only after he'd gotten into the Army and understood more about such things that Cole began to wonder if his family even owned the land that their shack was on. That far back in the woods, nobody bothered much with deeds or property lines. Coles had been living on that land since before the Revolutionary War, but it would be just like a Cole to be a squatter.

The shack was hammered together out of mismatched boards that very well might have gone missing from the side of someone's barn in the dead of night. Sheets of tin covered the roof, so spotted with rust that they resembled a Palomino hide.

Cole still remembered the first time that Hollis had wandered up to the shack, kicking the hounds out of the way, because he was one of the few visitors they'd ever had. With his gray hair and beard, Hollis had looked like an old man even back then. It turned out that he had seen the smoke from their chimney and gotten curious. He was their closest neighbor.

In his mind's eye, Cole could picture his mother greeting Hollis in her bare feet and threadbare dress. If it was warm out, Cole and his brothers didn't wear shirts or shoes. For a dress, one of his little sisters wore a flour sack with holes cut in it for her head and arms. Cole hadn't known any different then, but being in the Army had given him a new perspective on just how poor they'd been.

Old Hollis's eyes had never held a look of pity or of contempt. He had always greeted them with a warm smile, and once or twice, a stick of candy. There had even been a few times when a box of canned food was left on a stump near the start of the trail leading to the shack. Who would have left it but Hollis? No one else had ever given a damn about the Cole family. He turned up every now and then to buy deer antlers and buckskin off pa. He was never interested in buying any of pa's moonshine, which he called, "Devil spit."

* * *

ONCE COLE WAS OLD ENOUGH, it wasn't long before his wanderings took him out to Hollis Bailey's place. He'd heard that old Hollis was always on the lookout for scrap metal, and Cole had brought him whatever he could find. He reckoned it was an easier way to make money than trapping.

The neat, white farmhouse and red barn couldn't have been more different from the Cole family's shack. There was also the fact that Bailey's place lay within sight of the county road. The road wasn't paved, and it wasn't busy, but the occasional passing car or truck raised clouds of dust.

That first time, he'd found Hollis out in the barn.

"Why, if it ain't one of the Cole boys. How you gettin' along back there?"

Cole shrugged. "I reckon just fine, Mr. Bailey."

Hollis looked the skinny boy in front of him up and down, then sighed and patted the heavy leather apron he wore. Fine metal dust flew up and sparkled in the sun. "What can I do for you, boy? Looks like you got somethin' in that poke."

Cole did. He had been wandering the countryside, finding scraps of metal where he could. Basically, he gathered any metal that looked flat and straight enough to make a knife out of.

One by one, old man Hollis took the objects from the sack: leaf springs, broken farm implements, a couple of discarded discs off a seed drill. It looked like junk, but Hollis told him these were all good makings for knives.

"You been busy, ain't you, boy? I reckon these will do." He pulled the final piece of metal from the bag. Rusty as it was, the bar of metal appeared to be the least promising. Hollis smacked it against the woodpile to shake some of the rust off, then spat on a corner and worked the spit into the metal. "Huh, now where did you get this?"

"From up the mountain, sir. There was an old place there that burnt down a long time ago."

"That there is a special piece of metal," Hollis said, admiring the rusty metal. "That there is Damascus steel. They say some of the first settlers brought over metal like that. Mostly, we've lost the way of how to make it. Looks like you done found some."

He laid the metal almost delicately atop the rest of the pile.

"Pa said you buy metal."

"Normally, I pay cash money," Hollis said. "But I reckon you are the kind of boy who would give that money right over to his pa, like a boy should."

"Yes, sir."

What hung unspoken in the air was the fact that his pa would likely drink the money, or spend it on supplies to make moonshine.

Hollis rubbed his chin. "What if I was to pay you in canned goods? Maybe throw in a box of shells for that rifle of yours. You can tell your pa I'm short on cash money. Hell, cash money is as rare around here as an oyster."

Cole nodded. He had thought about hiding the money from his pa. This way was better.

From then on, Cole had visited old man Hollis from time to time. Sometimes he brought bits of metal, but just as often he simply liked to sit in the corner and watch the old man work. Hollis heated the metal in a rough-built forge near the barn, shaped the glowing metal by pounding it on an anvil, then polished it on a grinder that he turned by a foot treadle. The handles were wood or antler, often from the supply that Cole now brought periodically. Sometimes, Cole helped by holding a rough blade to the grindstone. If he ever survived this war, making knives was something he might consider doing.

Over the years, the bar of Damascus steel that Cole had found sat untouched on the shelf. Once, Cole had asked about it.

"Oh, that there is for somethin' special one of these days," Hollis said. "You only get one chance in a lifetime to make a knife like that."

* * *

COLE FINALLY REACHED into the box. In his hands, he now held the knife that Hollis had made from that bar of ancient Damascus steel. The blade was patterned after a Bowie knife, with the back side tapered and sharpened so that the blade formed a wicked point. The finger guard was brass and the handle made of antler from one of the bucks that Cole had hunted. As a rule, mountain people were more concerned about meat than trophy antlers, but whenever Cole had gotten a decent pair of antlers, he had taken them to Hollis.

The shape of the blade was one thing, but it was the blade itself that really captured the eye. The metal seemed to shift and change patterns as Cole turned the blade.

Something special, all right.

Studying the blade in Cole's hand, Vaccaro gave a low whistle.

"That is one beautiful knife. What are you going to do with it?"

"What do you think? I'm gonna make old Hollis proud that he sent me this knife."

Vaccaro shook his head. "And here I thought that it was a box of cookies. I ought to know by now that there's nothing sweet about you, Cole."

CHAPTER EIGHTEEN

ROHDE LAY awake in Lisette's bed, one hand cupping the girl's breast and his leg wedged between her warm thighs. He breathed in the girl's doughy feminine smell. They had fallen asleep after making love, but after that nap he found himself wide awake. While Rohde's body was pleasurably spent, his mind was now racing. He willed himself to go back to sleep, but it was like telling the wind to stop blowing.

He was thinking about the American hillbilly sniper.

It nagged at him that this hillbilly was still alive. One more bullet would finish off the American and cement Rohde's own reputation. Captain Fischer had said as much. But how did one find a single soldier in the vast battlefield?

Rohde thought that the best way might be to set a trap.

To lure a mouse into a trap, one needed cheese. To lure a lion, one needed a goat. To lure a man, one needed ... what, exactly?

That was the question Rohde contemplated as he lay awake in the girl's bed. He was supposed to be on patrol, plying his sniper's trade, and if anyone caught him here, he would surely be punished for dereliction of duty. He doubted that Fischer would have him shot, but who was to say? The punishment would depend upon the Hauptmann's mood.

Silently appraising the spent feeling in his loins and remembering their night of lovemaking, Rohde thought that each night he spent in Lisette's bed was well worth the risk.

Fortunately for him, being designated as a *Jäger* gave him a great deal of leeway and the ability to work alone. He was not the first German soldier who had slipped away to spend time with a French girl, nor was he likely to be the last, so long as the Allies had not yet driven German forces out of France.

Then Lisette would get herself an American boyfriend, or possibly a Frenchman. Rohde was nothing if not a realist.

He heard a vehicle on the road, coming fast, and he went tense all over. At this time of night it could only be a military vehicle. The curfew banned any travel by the French.

The vehicle sounded like a *Kubelwagen*, favored by officers and messengers. Headlights washed over the house as the vehicle went around a bend. He held his breath as the car drew even with the house, and then roared past.

Rohde breathed again.

He propped himself up on the pillow and lit a cigarette. It was a hot summer night so the windows were open. There were no screens on the farmhouse windows, but this far from the coast there didn't seem to be any mosquitoes. By day, of course, there were plenty of flies. Flies were a fact of farm life, especially in summer. The linen curtains waved in ghostly fashion in the slight breeze. Too hot for sheets or blankets.

From the room next door he heard the boy mumble in his sleep. Then all was quiet again. Lisette's niece and nephew were under strict orders to stay out of her room when he was there.

Starlight spilled through the window, giving a soft glow to the curves of Lisette's figure. She resembled a photograph taken in dim light. He gazed at her body in admiration, letting the image burn into his mind. Even though they had made love twice tonight, he felt a stirring that hinted at the possibility of a third time.

He recalled how the old men in the village would sigh at the sight of a pretty girl, and then gaze after her, lost in reverie. Was something like this what they were remembering? If he lived to be an old man, such an image might be a comfort someday, a reminder that he had lived a little and that he had been young once.

He hoped that his older brother had enjoyed some such comfort in his short life. Unlike the more prudish Allies, the SS and Wehrmacht often made informal arrangements for brothels to serve the troops.

Did you take a lover, Carl? I hope that you enjoyed that much, at least.

Until the death of his older brother, Rohde never had believed in heaven or any sort of life after death. He now hoped that there must, indeed, be something after this life. Otherwise, the finality of death overshadowed all the pleasure of living. Perhaps someday, he and Carl would be together once more, possibly in Valhalla, the hall of the gods where the dead enjoyed eternal feasting and camaraderie in the company of other heroes.

Maybe there really was a Valhalla? In the meantime, take joy where you can, he thought. His eyes wandered again to Lisette's naked body.

The cigarette was nearly smoked down, and he was thinking about lighting another, when he heard another vehicle on the road. This one was moving more slowly, feeling its way along the dark country road almost with stealth. He moved to the window and glanced out, but saw no headlights. Was it a military vehicle, he wondered, or something else? It was just possible that it might be a farmer moving illegal produce along the road, taking a huge chance. The price of breaking the curfew was a bullet in the head.

A French farmer did not worry him. But if it was a squad of SS on patrol—or worse yet, members of the French Resistance—he did not want to be caught in the house. The SS might very well shoot him and be done with it. However, the French *Maquis* would take their time cutting him into pieces with small, sharp knives, or perhaps torture him with hammers—he had heard rumors that this was their favorite implement to use on captured Germans. The thought made him shudder.

The French were nothing more than cowards, not real soldiers at all, but they were vicious all the same. With the advance of the Allies, and the Germans losing their grip on the countryside, the Resistance had grown bolder.

The vehicle was coming closer; he heard the engine slow as it approached the house. He didn't like the sound of that at all.

He moved away from the window and quickly tugged his clothes back on. His rifle was in a corner; he snatched it up before touching Lisette's shoulder. She only mumbled sleepily, so he shook her roughly until her eyes blinked awake.

On the road beyond the house, the vehicle came to a stop. The engine idled a moment, then switched off. He heard hushed male voices. They spoke French, which could only mean one thing.

"*Machi ici*," he said to Lisette, which was the best explanation he could give in French. He tried again in German, "The Resistance is here."

But Lisette had understood his broken French well enough. She sat bolt upright and pointed at her nightgown, flung on the back of a chair. Rohde grabbed it and tossed it at her.

Lisette peered out the window. "*Mon frere*," she whispered.

Lisette had explained that the children were her brother's and that he was away. *Away where?* Rohde had wanted to know. She had been vague on that point. Now, Rohde thought that he had the answer. Her brother must be a member of the Resistance. In the dead of night, her brother must have returned to see Lisette and his children. Rohde was sure now that the Frenchmen were not after him. There was no way that they even knew he was at the house.

Rohde intended to keep it that way. He did not even think of staying to fight. He did not like the odds, taking on an unknown number of Resistance fighters on their own territory. Lisette would just have to deal with her brother on her own. For her sake, Rohde hoped that her brother didn't figure out that Lisette had taken a German lover.

He straightened up from hurriedly tying his boots and gave Lisette a lopsided grin, then blew her a kiss. "*Au revoir*," he whispered, testing the limits of his French once more, then slipped out of the room, through the small farmhouse, past the useless old dog asleep in the farmhouse kitchen, and out the back door into the farmyard.

He was as silent as moonlight and shadow. Rohde hadn't survived as a sniper without possessing certain skills; by now, stealth was second nature.

He imagined his brother's ghost moving alongside him, keeping him company.

We make a good team, Carl. No one can hear us. We move like shadows in the night!

Moments later he was running across the farmyard. The humid night air was full of conflicting smells—honeysuckle, and the musky scent of some passing wild animal; the sweet scent of dewy grass being crushed under his boots, and then pungent manure.

He legged it across the next field toward the safety of the dark woods, the only sound coming from the long grass swishing against his legs. From the farmhouse, he finally heard the dog bark, then men's voices.

Rohde melted into the shadowy trees and was gone.

CHAPTER NINETEEN

BACK IN THE FARMHOUSE, feeling her way in the gloom of night, Lisette pulled on her nightgown and then fluffed the pillow that still held the shape of the young German soldier's head. She smoothed out the tangled sheets. She hoped that it would enough to erase any signs that Dieter had been there. The last thing that she wanted was for her brother to find any clue that a German soldier had been in her bed.

She felt ambivalent toward the German. What was he to her? To answer truthfully, he was more than any single thing. He was a lover, which she had never had before. It was a delicious secret to have a lover. And yet, she felt no actual *love* toward him. The feel of his body next to hers at night was pleasant, and she was sure that the German enjoyed every bit of what he had taken from her. But she sensed nothing like love from him, either. In the end, she decided that it was simply a bargain that had been struck between them, without any particular sentiment.

And then there was the more practical matter that the German soldier brought them food. Tins of rations, including canned meat. Chocolate. Even bread from the Wehrmacht bakeries that somehow still managed to operate even as the war closed in around them. Without the arrival of the German that day at their water pump, Lisette and the children would have gone hungry.

Thanks to the German, she and the children had been eating like barons for the past two weeks.

Their old dog finally heard the voices approaching from the road and barked a warning.

Lisette rushed into the kitchen, which a moment later was filled with the bulky figures of men. Their body odor was pronounced in the summer heat, new sweat layered on top of old. In the country where so few houses had running water, sweat was usually the familiar smell of honest toil, but she thought that she detected a tang of fear under it all. At any moment, they might be found out by the SS. The French weren't the only ones who patrolled the roads at night.

Her brother pushed forward. Even in the dark she recognized him. He was not a particularly tall man, but years of farm toil had made him strong. He took her by the shoulders, but they did not hug.

"Henri," she said. "Thank God you are safe."

Her brother did not bother to acknowledge her concern. She had the sense that he was making a show of bravado for the men. And yet, something in his face seemed different. He looked older, somehow, as if the last few weeks of fighting with the Resistance had hardened him. He was more than the simple farmer he had been.

"These men are hungry and thirsty," he said gruffly. "We dodged the Germans on the road twice just now."

"*Mon Dieu*," she said, well aware of the consequences of encountering a well-armed German patrol.

"We were too smart for those Germans. These are good men." Henri clapped a nearby man on the back and gave him a little push toward Lisette. "You remember Stefan from the village? He is with us."

Clearly, Henri wanted Lisette to notice Stefan. She found herself face to face with a vaguely familiar farm boy until he ducked away shyly.

"You must give these men something to eat," Henri ordered.

"We do not have much," Lisette heard herself say. "There is barely enough as it is."

"See that you fix them something," Henri said sharply. "Where are my children?"

"Wide awake and frightened in their beds, I'm sure," she responded, sounding more annoyed than she meant to. "Go see them, now that you have woken them up."

"I will."

Henri left, leaving her in the crowded kitchen. The men were unshaven, with hollow cheeks, as if they had been living rough in the woods and fields. The kitchen grew stifling with the smell of stale tobacco, old wine, and unwashed bodies.

She scrambled to give them something to eat. First, she brewed coffee and served it with lots of milk. At least there was plenty of that, though sugar for the coffee was scarce.

There was some bread that the German had brought. She sliced the bread and fried the slices in some bacon fat that she had been shepherding these last few weeks. The smell of food seemed to lift the spirits of the men, who began talking more freely to one another. They did not really include her in the conversation, however, but cast looks at her figure in the tight-fitting, worn dress when they thought she wasn't looking.

What else did she have to give them? A few eggs, which she broke, one by one, into the fat, and fried them just until the yolks had started to set. Still, it did not seem like enough. She thought of a can of chopped ham that the German had given her. She had been saving it, but these men seemed to need all the nourishment that she could spare. They were loyal Frenchmen, after all.

She took the can from the cabinet, opened it, and added the ham to the bread and eggs. She tossed the empty can into the midden pail.

It was a meager meal, but the four men accepted it gratefully. She saved a fifth plate for Henri, but did not eat anything herself, saving it for the men.

Henri returned in a few minutes, having tucked the children back into bed. He took his place at the crowded table and ate silently.

When they were finished, the men left their dirty plates at the table and went outside to smoke. Somehow, her precious bottle of red wine went out the door with them.

Henri stayed behind, watching as she cleared the table.

"You're eating better than I thought," he said ruefully. "Where did you get that canned ham? I would not have thought it was possible."

"I have been saving it," she said. "I thought your men could use it."

Finally, he stood and made his way to the midden pail, bent over, and held up the empty tin of canned ham, known as *Schinkenwurst*, the German equivalent of what Americans called Spam. The can was clearly stenciled with German markings.

"Where did you get this, Lisette?" he demanded in an accusing tone. Moving closer, he practically shoved the tin in her face.

She thought quickly, studying her brother's hard expression. She had coached the children to keep Dieter's visits a secret, but she wondered if they had let that secret slip. Was it possible that Henri now knew the truth and was only trying to catch her in a lie? "I traded some eggs for it," she said.

"You traded with *Germans*?" Henri nearly spat the last word. "Lisette, what are you thinking? They are the enemy."

Lisette felt relieved that her secret was safe—so far. Yet she was still indignant. "What can I say? The children and I need to eat. It is only a little tin of meat, hardly enough to feed us, let alone you and your friends."

"They are not friends," he corrected her. "They are soldiers fighting for a free France."

Try as she might, Lisette could not equate these shabby, leering men with heroes. "If you say so."

"I do say so," he said. He caught her wrist, squeezing it painfully. He pressed the empty ration can closer to her face, filling her nose with the metallic odor of factory-processed meat. "Listen to me, Lisette. You are playing a dangerous game. Stay away from the Germans. First you start trading eggs, but then who knows what else you might start trading with them? You should see how the girls who collaborated with the Germans are being treated in the areas that have been liberated. I would not want to see that happen to my sister."

Having made his point, he released his grip.

Lisette snatched back her hand and rubbed her wrist. She could only imagine how angry Henri would be if he knew the truth about her German lover.

Glaring at her, Henri tossed the empty tin back in the midden pail.

He had expected her to be cowed, but Lisette found herself struggling to control her growing anger. She was no longer the little sister that she had been before he left. Henri started to leave the kitchen, but she blocked his path.

"Listen to you, Henri! You go away for a few weeks and suddenly you are full of wisdom? Now you are a hero of

France? Let me tell you how it is. You left me here alone to tend this farm and your children. What am I to feed them? None of the neighbors bring me food! They have little enough for themselves. What have you brought me tonight but grief and more mouths to feed?"

If Henri had been angry before, the look of rage brought on by her outburst was all too clear. She stared in disbelief at his raised hand. He slapped her so hard that Lisette staggered back against the sink.

"You don't know what you are saying!" he shouted. Spittle flew from his lips. She had never seen him so angry. "You have not seen the things that I have seen these last few weeks, or done the things that I have done. When I tell you to stay away from the Germans, you had better listen unless you want to end up with a shaved head, or worse!"

"What could be worse?"

"In some places they are banishing the girls who took up with the Germans. Sometimes they are beaten to within an inch of their lives. Is that what you want, Lisette?"

Finally, he dodged around her and headed out the door to join his companions, smoking their cigarettes in the dooryard. Passing around her bottle of wine. The shy one named Stefan gave her a furtive look, like a rat eying the cheese.

Lisette's cheek stung, but one did not grow up on a farm without enduring pain from time to time. This was nothing. She stayed behind in the kitchen, to clean up the mess that her brother and the other men had made. *The story of my life*, she thought.

She just hoped that she could continue to keep Dieter's visits a secret from Henri. The war had changed him. What might Henri be capable of, if he discovered the truth about her German soldier? Would he stand by if she was punished in public, or would he join in?

CHAPTER TWENTY

Rohde dodged a couple of SS patrols out looking for French Resistance fighters or perhaps American commandos and made it back to the command post in time for a few hours of sleep.

He was up even earlier than usual on that August morning. Not so much as a hint of sunrise had touched the horizon and no birds sang. The air was heavy with dew and smelled of wet grass and plowed earth. Rohde liked mornings because they were full of promise.

He relieved himself in the slit trench near the command post. After a moment's reflection, he took with him the short-handled camp shovel that had been stuck into a pile of earth to freshen the latrine from time to time. He would need the shovel for what he had planned.

He went back and retrieved his rifle, then took the Zeiss telescopic sight from its protective wooden box and mounted it to the K98. He double-checked the mounts, satisfied that the rifle was ready for action. Rohde's last piece of equipment for the day was a bayonet that he liberated from a bunkmate's gear. There was little use for bayonets on the battlefield, but the 18-inch blade would be perfect for what Rohde had in mind.

He stopped at the barn that served as the unit's mess. There, he grabbed a quick cup of coffee and a roll. A few sleepy men were already starting the business of the day, but none of them so much as acknowledged Rohde.

He hardly noticed that Scheider was not there. Rohde felt no regrets. Scheider had thought that Rohde had let slip some nugget and had been only too eager to ambush the American unit on the road to St. Dennis de Mere. He had not counted on the American sniper coming along, but then again, neither had Rohde.

"Has it gotten so bad that snipers have to dig their own graves now, eh, Rohde?"

He looked up from his coffee and roll in surprise to see that it was the armorer, Hohenfeldt, who had spoken. The armorer pointed at the camp shovel propped against the bench where Rohde sat, then raised his coffee mug in salute, as if it were a beer stein. The slight sneer and tone of his voice belied the gesture. "You are up very early. It is good to see that you are so eager to get busy shooting Amis. You are getting quite the reputation."

"No thanks to you," Rohde said.

"Whatever do you mean?" Hohenfeldt asked with an air of mock innocence.

"I might not have to get up so early if you would just give me that damn Gewehr 43 you're so attached to."

Hohenfeldt snorted. "I am not the only one attached to something. I hear that you are quite attached to some French girl in the countryside nearby."

Rohde paused with a chunk of bread halfway to his mouth. "That is none of your damn business."

Where in the world had Hohenfeldt heard about Lisette? Rohde knew well that you were never really alone in the countryside. Sentries and patrols might have seen him coming and going from Lisette's place. Soldiers loved to gossip. It was not against regulations to have a French girlfriend. Visiting her when he should have been on duty was another matter, however.

"I only make the point that you have your girlfriend, and I have my rifle."

"They are hardly one and the same," Rohde said.

"Maybe, and maybe not," he said. Hohenfeldt fixed him with a knowing smile and pushed back from the table, preparing to leave. "You just let me know if you ever want to trade."

Rohde watched the armory sergeant go, without comment. Old Hohenfeldt could be trying to undermine him somehow, or he could just be busting his balls—annoying, to be sure, but ultimately harmless. The question was, which game was Hohenfeldt playing at?

Rohde had no time to think about that now. He wanted to get out in the field under cover of darkness. Hohenfeldt had been right when he'd said that Rohde wanted to get busy hunting Americans. What he did not know was that Rohde had one particular American in mind.

The hillbilly sniper.

He shouldered his rifle and trudged away from the command post in the pre-dawn light. The few sentries that he passed mumbled a greeting or simply nodded at him. Within twenty minutes he had left the more secure areas behind and was in the countryside. The Americans had not penetrated this far yet in their advance. Not yet, at any rate. In other day or two, they would be reaching this territory.

When they did, Rohde would be waiting.

He began to scrutinize his surroundings with the practiced eye of a sniper. Trees grew at intervals along the roads, and any one of them would have made a good perch. He paid special attention to the farm buildings he passed, mostly small cottages and stone barns, seeking out the advantages of each one, and just as quickly dismissing them. Instinctively, Rohde wished to avoid trees or buildings. He did not wish to become trapped, but preferred open country where he could move.

He pressed on, moving deeper into the countryside as the light grew in the east. The red rim of the sun appeared on the horizon like a bloodshot eye. The landscape was still full of shadows, and if any hostile eyes were watching, his camouflage uniform enabled him to pass through relatively unseen.

Rohde soon found what he was looking for. He found one such field, perhaps measuring 25 hectares and ringed by a scrubby hedgerow, out of which grew a few taller trees. Judging by the tall grass, this seemed to be a hay field. The war had created a shortage of farm workers, and this field had not been kept as tidy as it should. Brush and tall weeds encroached from a corner near the hedgerow, where it was difficult for the horse-drawn scythe to reach, and the field had gone untended. The farmer's loss was Rohde's gain.

The fields here near Argentan were much larger than the ones nearer to Normandy. Anyone crossing this field would be badly exposed. Praying that no enemy snipers were about, Rohde stepped into the field to get his bearings.

To catch a mouse, one needed cheese ...

As a general rule, a sniper did not have the luxury of creating his hide, but had to adapt to his surroundings. He had to blend into them to be most effective.

He remembered the test they had been given during sniper training. The trainees were sent out into a no-man's land. There, they were told to set up their hides. The instructor kept watch, and anyone he saw was "out"—in combat, they would have been dead, picked off by the enemy. Rohde had dug himself a shallow hole and managed to stay hidden until the instructor had called them in. Rohde had turned out to be one of the last men who had managed to stay hidden from the instructor's eyes. Fortunately, he had drank little and eaten sparingly that morning. The lesson had been simple, but it had stuck with Rohde. Beyond a rifle, a sniper's best friends were a shovel and patience.

Now that more of the sun was showing through the trees beyond the field, Rohde had enough light to get to work. He placed the rifle within easy reach. Stuck in his belt was the camp shovel. He took it out now and began to dig.

Though the morning was cool, his muscles soon warmed to the work. Breaking through the tangled mesh of roots in the field caused him to break out into an actual sweat. He ended up cutting out blocks of sod and setting them aside. The rich soil itself was easy to remove, and he scattered the shoveled earth across the field so that there would be no telltale piles of soil. Soon, he had shoveled out a depression just deep enough and long enough to hide him from sight.

He stretched out in the hole, then used the shovel to notch out a bit more space for his elbows. Satisfied, he climbed out, brushed off the dirt, and went to work on a narrow trench back toward where brush and shrubs marched out from the hedgerow.

The distance wasn't more than 10 meters, but it was still backbreaking work to cut through the sod with the short-handled camp shovel. Rohde wished that he had thought to bring along a mattock as well. Fortunately, the ditch did not need to be particularly deep. He just needed it to be deep enough that he could writhe his way through it on his elbows and knees. The tall grass would provide the rest of the camouflage.

He cut the ditch toward a clump of multiflora rose. The thick, thorny canes made excellent cover, and yet, through a gap in the rose bush, Rohde had a clear view of the field.

He straightened up and stretched out his back, stiff from digging, and walked toward the hedgerow. There, he spent several minutes hunting for just what he needed—a stout forked branch. He used the bayonet to chop a rough point at the long end and then used the flat of the shovel to drive the branch into the earth in front of the gap in the rose bush. He now had a sturdy rest for his rifle.

That left the final stretch between the rose bush and the hedgerow itself. Rohde took the bayonet and walked some distance away, then began hacking down branches and brush. He dragged them back and used the material to create a screen between the rose bush and the hedgerow. He should be able to move relatively unseen behind it.

Satisfied, he found a gap in the hedgerow itself. At the heart of the hedgerow was an ancient wall made of stone and earth. Trees and brush had grown up around it, anchored by the wall deep within the hedgerow's interior. Rohde burrowed inside the tangled growth until he reached the wall. There was a large, flat stone that made an excellent bench rest. He was able to position himself behind it. With the rifle laid across the stone, he had a solid platform from which to shoot. The view of the field was somewhat obscured by the overhanging branches and wooded growth, but the elevation of the wall offered its own advantages. Also, the vegetation would screen him from the enemy, in that it was easier for him to see out than to be seen within.

Satisfied with his work, he remained hidden inside the hedge long enough to drink half his canteen of water and then smoke a cigarette. The sun was higher now, starting to touch the treetops and reach across the grass. Birds flitted everywhere.

A flash of movement on the ground caught his eye and Rohde reached for his rifle. But he saw that it was only a chipmunk. Nature went about its business, oblivious to the war.

He shook his head, chiding himself for being so careless. He had become so caught up in the work that he had let his guard down. If some enemy soldier had come upon him, Rohde would already be dead. That would have been an ignoble end to his sniping career, to die with a shovel in his hand. He smoked another cigarette, but this time he kept his grip on the rifle.

Rohde's series of holes, ditches, and brush was not exactly elegant, but it was certainly more elaborate than any series of hides he had created before. None of it qualified as any great feat of engineering or even of sniper craft. However, the fact that he had created three separate fallbacks here at the edge of the field went beyond anything he had done before.

To trap a lion, one needed a goat.

Now, all that he needed was the bait. He had just the thing in mind.

CHAPTER TWENTY-ONE

LATER THAT DAY, Rohde found Hohenfeldt at work, supervising a couple of teenaged *Soldaten* taking inventory of the ammunition stocks. The *Stabsfeldwebel* looked on, clipboard balanced on his heavy belly, sweat dripping off him in the airless tent, as the two *Soldaten*, shirtless in the heat and slick with sweat, climbed among the stacked crates and called numbers out to him. With camouflaged netting draped over the tent, the air was very close, and the interior of the tent smelled strongly of sweat, sawdust from the ammo crates, and gun oil.

He glanced around for the Gewehr 43, but it was nowhere in sight. That damn old *Stabsfeldwebel* had hidden it away.

Rohde was determined to get his hands on that Gewehr 43. He would take every advantage that he could as a sniper, and that included a superior weapon. The thought of the American hillbilly sniper loomed large in his mind. Having triumphed over the American sniper once before, he was certain that he could do it again. It would help if he had a new semi-automatic rifle. Having laid his trap, and armed with the Gewehr, all he would have to do was lure in the American sniper.

With the Allied troops about to bear down on the German positions around Perle des Champs, it made sense that every last Panzerfaust and round of 7.92 mm ammunition be accounted for. Already, the troops were being issued extra ammunition beyond the standard 65 rounds. Some grumbled about it because of the added weight, but those who had been in combat previously knew better than to complain about carrying extra clips of ammo. Soon enough, every bullet might count. The more experienced soldiers crammed every pocket full of ammo.

It was not a lack of ammunition that was causing problems for the Germans, but a lack of air power. On the ground, the Germans had the training and the firepower to hold off twice their number. The Germans sold each acre of French territory dearly. But from the air, they were vulnerable.

"Hey, Hohenfeldt," Rohde called to get the *Stabsfeldwebel*'s attention.

Hohenfeldt turned around and acknowledged Rohde with a put-upon expression. "You don't give up, do you, Rohde? You are still after that rifle. The answer is no. Anyhow, can't you see that I'm busy?"

"Those two poor bastards look busy. Are you trying to give them heat stroke? You look like you're standing around."

"Rohde, it goes without saying that I am a *Stabsfeldwebel* and you are a *Gefreiter*. Which means that I outrank you. So piss off, unless you want to help count boxes."

Hohenfeldt turned his attention back to the clipboard. Rohde did not care to be so easily dismissed. He considered how gratifying it would be to put a bullet hole through Hohenfeldt's broad forehead, which was wrinkled now in concentration.

"I am not here to count bullets for you, *Staber*. I want to talk to you about getting hold of that rifle."

Hohenfeldt sighed audibly. "Get out of here, Rohde!"

"Come now, don't be that way. I think that you will want to hear what I have to say."

"Then what are you waiting for? Say it."

Rohde gave the two sweating soldiers a significant look. "Let's go have a cigarette."

Hohenfeldt couldn't help but be curious. He barked some orders at the two soldiers, and then followed Rohde outside.

Rohde lit a cigarette and offered the pack to Hohenfeldt, who considered it as if it might be booby-trapped, then shook out a cigarette and accepted a light from Rohde.

"What?" he asked, exhaling smoke through teeth stained yellow by nicotine and coffee. He sat down on a box and his whole body sagged. Hohenfeldt was not a model specimen of a German soldier. "Hurry up. I have things to do."

"I want that rifle," Rohde said.

"And I want a box of chocolates and a feather bed." He laughed. "I want a French girl to fondle my balls."

"There, you see? We all want something. What if I could get you something that you want, Hohenfeldt?"

Hohenfeldt's eyes narrowed. "This is tricky territory, Rohde. Are you trying to bribe me? That is not how I run my armory."

"Of course not, Herr Stabsfeldwebel. That would be against regulations. No, what I am offering you is a favor between friends."

Hohenfeldt inhaled deeply, held the smoke, then exhaled. "What did you have in mind?"

"I thought you might enjoy a visit with my French girl. That is, unless you would rather stand around watching these two sweaty boys."

"A visit?"

"A roll in the hay."

"And what does this girl think of that?"

"Don't worry about what she thinks. She will do what I tell her."

Hohenfeldt was thinking about it, trying to find the downside of the bargain. Rohde could almost imagine the gear's turning behind his rheumy eyes. In Hohenfeldt's case, it was more like the cycling of a well-oiled weapon. "When?" he asked.

"Tonight. I will meet you here and we can walk over to her farm."

The armorer finally nodded. Then he actually licked his lips as if in anticipation of what was to come that night. "I hope that you are not planning to make a fool of me, or you will be sorry, Rohde."

Rohde turned to go, then stopped and said, "I will hold up my end of the bargain, *Staber*. You just be sure to have that rifle for me, or you will be the one who is sorry."

* * *

AT MIDNIGHT he met Hohenfeldt as agreed and brought him around to Lisette's farmhouse. He would have liked to walk, silent in the velvety night, but Hohenfeldt was having none of that. The armorer complained that his knees ached too much to walk the entire distance. They took a motorcycle instead, with Hohenfeldt stuffed into the sidecar. Never mind the fact that the countryside might be crawling with *Machi* fighters and possibly with Allied scouts. Any of them would be happy to cut their throats, and the loud engine made them a target.

They drove down the country roads with the headlight off, just in case there were any Allied aircraft lurking above. Between their slow progress and the loud motor, Rohde was sure that they would be ambushed at every curve and copse. By some miracle, they made it to the farmhouse.

Lisette emerged to greet them, her old dog hanging around her knees, barking.

"Who's this?" she asked, puzzled.

"An old friend of mine," Rohde said. "He wanted to meet you."

The *Stabsfeldwebel* hardly did more than take off his hat and nod. Rohde steered him toward a chair and announced, "I will be right back."

He left them in the kitchen, staring awkwardly at one another. Hohenfeldt, like Rohde himself, spoke almost no French and Lisette knew only a smattering of German.

Rohde knew that what he was doing was monstrous and that Lisette would never forgive him. But tonight, he was thinking only in practical terms. Allied troops would soon reach this sector, and that would put an end to their affair. At most, they had another night or two together and would likely never see one another again. Rohde was willing to trade those remaining nights for the rifle that old Hohenfeldt had refused to give him until now.

But how would he ever get Lisette to go along with him?

The cottage was very small, and in two steps he had entered the twins' bedroom. They were only half asleep, the commotion of Rohde and Hohenfeldt's arrival on the motorcycle having awakened them. He scooped them up, balancing one sleepy child on each hip, and returned to the kitchen. Hohenfeldt hadn't budged from the chair, grinning at Lisette.

Lisette watched with uncertainty, and then growing alarm, as Rohde entered the kitchen. Perhaps she had read his intentions in his face. The twins were oblivious and slumped against him sleepily. He never really interacted with them, but by now, they were used to his presence.

"*Suce sa bite*," he said, nodding at Hohenfeldt.

Rohde knew the French phrase was crude and harsh. All at once, the enormity of what he was asking seemed to dawn on Lisette. She stood up, her face angry, and it was hard to say what she planned to do next. Then her gaze fell upon the children that Rohde was holding.

He jerked his chin from Hohenfeldt to the bedroom. Then he gave the little girl a peck on the head. His meaning was all too clear. Some small part of Rohde hated himself for what he was doing, but it seemed like the best way to control Lisette.

By now, Lisette was shaking with fear and anger. He could see emotion racing across her face. Her eyes struck at him like daggers. But what choice did she have?

She hissed a single word at him, "*Monstre.*" Monster.

If he felt anything at that moment, he pushed it aside.

She shot a hateful look at Rohde, then turned and made her way down the short hallway to her bedroom. Hohenfeldt followed, crowding close behind. He was a tall man, and fairly wide, so there was no way Lisette was getting past him. They went into the bedroom and shut the door.

Rohde doubted that Hohenfeldt would take long. The children seemed unconcerned about anything that was happening. He returned the little girl to her bed and tucked her in, giving her a piece of chocolate in the process. He had other plans for Leo.

"Would you like to go on an adventure?" he asked the boy in broken French.

The girl spoke up. "*Je voudrais partir à l'aventure!*"

"*Les garçons seulement.* This is for boys only. Leo?"

When Leo nodded, wide-eyed, Rohde carried him out and put him into the motorcycle sidecar. Then he gave the boy a piece of chocolate to keep him occupied.

When Hohenfeldt came out a few minutes later, he was surprised that he had to share the sidecar with the boy. Somehow, they both managed to squeeze in. The boy had to sit in his lap. Given the fact that Hohenfeldt was whistling, he was in too good of a mood to complain.

"Don't worry, Rohde. I showed your girl a trick or two."

"Go to hell, *Staber*." Rohde hated him for making him trade Lisette for the rifle.

Hohenfeldt chuckled. The *Staber* seemed to find the night's events amusing. He sat in the sidecar, licking his lips like the cat that had eaten the canary.

CHAPTER TWENTY-TWO

THEIR LAST STOP of the night was the armory. With Rohde having fulfilled his end of the bargain, it was time for the *Staber* to do the same. He left the boy in the sidecar, pointing at him sternly and stating, "*Ici*."

"I can't imagine what you want with that boy," the Staber said. "You ought to have left him at home."

"This is coming from the man who just screwed the boy's aunt. What wonderful concern you have shown."

"I do feel bad for the aunt, you know. I feel bad for her when she has to make do with you."

"You are an asshole, Hohenfeldt."

The *Staber* just laughed. "That's asshole, *sir*, to you. Do you want that rifle or not? If you do, then come inside."

Seething now, Rohde followed him in. The *Staber* went to his makeshift but neat office area. He watched as Hohenfeldt retrieved a bundle that he had tucked between the desk and the wall. With deft hands used to working with guns, the *Staber* unwrapped the oily cloth to reveal the Gewehr 43. Much to Rohde's chagrin, he realized that the *Staber* had hidden the rifle rather than storing it with the other small arms, most likely to keep Rohde from stealing it. The *Staber* was nothing if not wily. He certainly had not trusted Rohde.

Rohde examined the rifle. This particular weapon was equipped with a Zielfernrohr 43 (ZF 4) telescopic sight with 4x magnification. The *Staber* slapped a 10-round magazine on the desk. The weapon used the same 7.92 mm ammunition as the Mauser K98. The wood was stained lighter than the standard issue Mausers.

Even at first glance, it was a much different weapon from the Mauser K98 in that it was not nearly so finely made. The Mauser had benefitted from years of design evolution. The new rifle was at least 5 cm shorter. There was none of the Mauser's silky smooth metal. The metal parts still had rough edges and stamp parts on them, as if the weapon had been hastily made, thrown together in some factory between air raids.

The stock had a chunky look about it, as if it had been carved from a rectangle of wood with the least effort possible, and encased all but the last 10 centimeters of the barrel. In this regard, the rudimentary stock resembled some of the Russian rifles that Rohde had seen. The butt plate appeared to be made from a thick chunk of iron. The overall impression was of a very sturdy weapon that could double as a club.

What the rifle lacked in form, it made up for in function. And there was no denying that the Gewehr 43 functioned very well. Its simple gas piston operation had been copied from captured Russian rifles and then improved upon by German gunsmiths. The result was a highly accurate rifle with an impressive rate of fire.

"This one was made in Lübeck. It is zeroed in for 200 meters. With the scope, that gets one to an effective range of around 800 meters," Hohenfeldt said. He gave Rohde a doubtful look. "Maybe less in your case."

"Go to hell."

"With the 10-round magazines, you can fire maybe forty rounds a minute if you aren't so worried about what you are hitting."

Rohde was impressed. Compared to his bolt-action Mauser, the rate of fire was maybe 3 to 1.

Hohenfeldt held out his hands, as if to take the rifle back.

"What? It's mine now."

"I cannot issue you a new rifle until you return your old one."

Rohde held the rifle closer, and grabbed the spare magazines off the desk. If they'd had any bullets in them, he might have tried out the rifle on Hohenfeldt.

"I am taking this with me tonight."

"Suit yourself, but you had better turn in your Mauser first thing in the morning. If you do not, I will report you to Hauptmann Fischer."

Rohde ground his teeth. "I will have that back in the morning. Good night, *Staber*."

"And good night to you, Rohde. You can be sure I will have some pleasant dreams about your French girl, ha, ha!"

* * *

ROHDE SLEPT FITFULLY, thinking about the trap he would set in the morning. He glanced over at Lisette's nephew, Leo, wrapped in a thin blanket on the floor beside Rohde's cot. The boy still thought that he was having a grand adventure.

He was well aware that Leo might never be returning home. He was equally aware that while Lisette would never forgive him for whoring her out to old Hohenfeldt, she would hate him with all her being for kidnapping her nephew. He pushed any thoughts of guilt or remorse from his mind. This was war. One did what one must.

All that mattered now was that he had the new rifle. And he had the bait.

Now, he needed the quarry.

To trap a lion, one needed a goat.

Rohde's fitful sleep was not helped by the fact that he could hear artillery that was getting too close for comfort as the Allies closed in on Perle des Champs. The whole world as he had known it these last few months was about to end.

He just needed a day or two to enact his plan. Once the American hillbilly sniper was dead, he could escape with the other German forces across the Rhine, to make their last stand in the Fatherland.

Rohde did finally nod off, but it seemed like only a few minutes later that he awoke in the pre-dawn darkness. Time to get up and get going. It was going to be a busy day.

He glanced down at Leo and saw that the boy was still sleeping deeply. Rohde debated for a moment, and then decided to leave him there for now. Chances were that the boy would not wake until Rohde roused him.

Rohde dressed quickly, then picked up his old sniper rifle, the Mauser K98. He had debated whether to bother returning it to the armory, but decided that it was better if that fat bastard Hohenfeldt had no reason to make trouble for him.

With the rifle in hand, he made his way to the armory.

To his surprise, the *Stabsfeldwebel* was not there. Instead, he found a sleepy-eyed *Soldat* on duty, one of the same ones who had been shifting boxes yesterday. Rohde considered himself to be young, but he felt positively geriatric compared to this skinny *Soldat*. Lately, young boys of no more than fifteen or sixteen years old were being sent to fill the ranks.

"Where is the *Staber*?" Rohde asked.

"He is not here," the *Soldat* explained. When Rohde's

glare told him that he had stated the obvious, the boy added, "Gone to take a shit, most likely."

That was no surprise. Hohenfeldt liked to brag about the regularity of his bowels in the morning. He seemed to feel that it was a good quality in a soldier.

Rohde hefted the Mauser. "He told me to leave him this. I will just put it on his desk."

The *Soldat* shrugged. Rohde made his way over to Hohenfeldt's desk. He did not have a separate office, but had partially screened his desk area by arranging stacks of crates around it.

Rohde propped the rifle against the desk, looking up to note that the *Soldat* on duty could not see him. He took the opportunity to snoop, taking some small measure of satisfaction from invading the Hohenfedlt's workspace.

Not that there was much to see. The desk was orderly, with neat stacks of requisition forms, a black Bakelite phone connected to the Wehrmacht telephone grid, and three neatly sharpened pencils set out side by side.

Also on the desk was a locket that he had seen Lisette wear. Surely, she would not have given it to Hohenfeldt. The Staber must have taken it as a kind of prize. For some reason, the sight of the stolen locket made Rohde see red. It was nothing more than a cheap drugstore locket, but must have been one of the few pieces of jewelry that the girl owned. Hadn't the *Staber* already taken enough, just so that Rohde could get his hands on that damn rifle? To Rohde, taking the locket just seemed greedy. He left the locket where it lay.

There was still no sign of Hohenfeldt or of the *Soldat*, so Rohde opened the desk drawers. The large side drawers contained nothing more than blank forms. A bottle of schnapps shared space with the forms in the bottom drawer.

The top desk drawer proved more interesting. He found a mostly full pack of fancy gold-tipped French cigarettes and pocketed that. That would annoy Hohenfeldt later, no doubt. But what caught his attention was a small double-barreled derringer.

Rohde picked it up and examined the derringer. The entire pistol fit neatly into his hand. Finely made with a polished wooden stock and filigreed scrollwork, it was just the sort of weapon that a gentleman might keep in a drawer of his study or in a bedside table, as protection against night-time burglars. Who knew where the Staber had come across it. Though useless as a military weapon, Rohde could understand why the Staber had kept it in his desk as a kind of novelty piece. It was a beautiful little weapon from another era.

He slid the catch and opened the action. Two fresh shell casings winked back at him, like brass eyes. The derringer was novel, but deadly.

Rohde slipped the derringer into his pocket.

The *Soldat* barely noticed him go out.

Rohde had intended to head back to the barrack to collect the boy and head out into the field, but he found that his feet carried him towards the latrine area. He wasn't even sure what he had in mind, other than the fact that his right hand was thrust into his trouser pocket, wrapped around the derringer.

It was early, and the latrine area was still dark, but easily identifiable by its smell. A bench seat had been constructed over the ditch for some level of comfort. The figure squatting on it had to be Hohenfeldt.

Rohde walked over to him, and the *Staber* looked up at him in surprise.

"Rohde? What are you doing here? Don't tell me that you tracked me down to complain about the Gewehr. If you want more bullets, you'll have to arrange another visit for me with your girlfriend."

"That's not going to happen, you fat piece of shit. I should have done this a long time ago."

Rohde took the derringer out of his pocket and leveled it at Hohenfeldt's face. Even in the dim light, he could see the *Staber's* eyes get very big. The gun went off with a pop, sending a few grams of lead crashing into the *Staber's* forehead and turning his brain to sausage. The big man made an "Oh" sound like all the air going out of a tire, and slumped over on the bench. Rohde felt such a wave of hatred for Hohenfeldt that it was only with an effort that he refrained from shooting him with the second barrel. Instead, he wrapped the *Staber's* right hand around the derringer.

With any luck, the *Staber's* death would be seen as a suicide. More than one depressed soldier had chosen a bullet as a form of escape, but ending one's life in the company latrine had to be a first. The question was, would anyone believe it?

One thing Rohde did know for certain was that the fat old bastard would not be missed.

The pop of the derringer had not gone unnoticed. Rohde heard a shout and the sound of running footsteps. But he was long gone before anyone arrived.

CHAPTER TWENTY-THREE

ONCE THE FAT sergeant had finished with her, Lisette scrubbed herself in the basin of water in the corner of the bedroom. The cottage had no running water, so this was the age-old method of cleaning up. Wherever the German had touched her, she rubbed until her skin was raw. The pain of it felt good, almost as if she was punishing herself, although she had done nothing wrong.

Out in the yard, she heard a motorcycle start up, and then motor off. That would be that bastard, Dieter, driving off with that sack of meat he had brought along tonight. The sound of the motorcycle faded, but the noise of artillery seemed to have grown louder and had not abated much by nightfall.

Dieter. The name tasted sour in her mouth. She had not been fond of him, well aware that he was a German, but they'd had an agreeable business arrangement. He was a young man far from home, and she was a young woman with mouths to feed. It was one thing to trade her body for food. Whoring her out to another man had gone too far. If she ever saw him again, she would take the ancient shotgun in the kitchen and shoot him. She did not care if he was a sniper.

Satisfied that she was as clean as she was going to get, she headed to the children's bedroom. She could make out her niece's sleeping form. Somehow, her niece had managed to get back into bed and go right to sleep as if nothing had happened.

When she looked at Leo's bed, however, the boy was not there.

Lisette felt her heart skip in her chest. Dieter and the fat German sergeant had not frightened her, but the sight of that empty bed did. Where had her nephew gone?

She went into the kitchen, then wandered back to her own bedroom, and then to the twins' bedroom again. The house was too small for Leo to be hiding anywhere.

Lisette ran into the farmyard, calling his name. "Leo? Leo? Where are you?"

She checked the outhouse. Then the barn and henhouse. Nothing.

It would not have been like her nephew to wander off. He had certainly never done that before, and he would not have done that at night, alone.

Lisette recalled the sound of the motorcycle fading in the night. With a sinking feeling, she realized that Dieter and the German sergeant had not left alone. She could not think of any other explanation for Leo's disappearance. For whatever reason, they must have taken Leo with them.

* * *

LISETTE DID NOT GO BACK to bed. Sleep would have been impossible. She made coffee and sat at the kitchen table until first light, deciding what to do, and hoping against hope that

Leo would come wandering in from some hiding place. Maybe he had been scared by the Germans.

The chickens stirred, the rooster crowed, and Lisette remained alone.

She wished she knew where her brother, Henri, had gone. She could have used his help. But like so many young Frenchmen, he was off fighting the Germans, prying their fingers away from France. That was all well and good, but what about the children?

Getting Leo back was up to her, and her alone.

She would have to confront the Germans at their headquarters to do it. The thought of that filled her with trepidation.

Lisette knew that she could not take Elsa with her. She was walking into the lion's den, after all. There was a good chance that she would not be coming back. With the Germans, there was no telling what might happen.

Her mind made up, Lisette went and woke up Elsa. She gave the girl bread and a cup of milk for breakfast. When Lisette questioned her, it was clear that Elsa had no idea what had become of her brother, nor did she seem especially frightened by what had happened last night.

"Dieter gave me chocolate," she announced. A pout soon replaced her smile. "He said he was taking Leo on an adventure. I wanted to go, but he said it was for boys only."

Lisette could only nod at her niece's childish innocence. "Drink your milk."

"What is wrong, *Tante*?"

"I must go find Leo. Did anyone say where this adventure was going to be?"

Elsa just shrugged.

There was an old woman named Madame Pelletier who lived half a mile away. Leaving Elsa alone with her bread and milk, Lisette left long enough to bring back the old woman. She agreed to mind Elsa at the house. Lisette wanted someone there, just in case Leo returned on his own, by some miracle.

She scribbled a quick note to Henri, explaining what she was doing. She did not go into detail, of course; Henri would blame her more than the Germans for what had happened. She left instructions with Madame Pelletier to tell Henri where she had gone, if he happened to appear.

"If I can, I will call you," she said, nodding at the old telephone on the wall. By some miracle, it still worked—say what you wanted about the Germans, but the roads, electricity, and telephone service had vastly improved during their occupation of France. Her farmhouse was close enough to the road for a telephone; old Madame Pelletier's house didn't have one yet.

Upon leaving the cottage, Lisette's first thought was to visit German headquarters. Leo might be there, and perhaps she could lodge a complaint against Rohde—for all the good that it would do. The Germans could care less what French civilians thought.

However, she had not gone far when a vehicle came up the road. She had been expecting a German truck and was taken aback by the large white star on the hood. Americans!

The truck slowed. The sight of a young French girl, walking alone down a road, was enough to get the attention of the soldiers in the truck.

"Need a ride, miss?" the driver asked enthusiastically. He spoke French with a very heavy accent, but was understandable.

Quickly, Lisette explained about her missing nephew. She had to tell her story three times, ever more slowly, before the driver understood it all. The driver then told her in no uncertain terms that she would never make it to German headquarters. There was already heavy fighting in that direction. The Germans, he said, were surrounded.

Lisette's heart sank, thinking of Leo.

"If I were you, I'd try our forward command post. If anyone found a kid, that's where he'd be. Hop in. We're headed there right now."

Lisette thought that made more sense than finding herself in the middle of a battlefield, or than searching aimlessly across the woods and fields. There was also the unsettling thought that if she found Leo, she might also come upon Dieter Rohde. If that happened, it might be useful to be accompanied by soldiers. The GIs eagerly made room for her in the cab of the truck, and off they went.

CHAPTER TWENTY-FOUR

WELL BEFORE DAWN THAT MORNING, Rohde was back in the field where he had prepared his sniper's hides. In the gloom, he looked them over quickly and saw with satisfaction that everything from the hole in the field, to his makeshift shooting blind, to his shooting platform within the hedgerow itself, blended almost perfectly into the landscape. It would take a sniper with the eyes of a hawk to spot anything amiss.

Rohde realized that he did not feel the least bit of guilt about shooting Hohenfeldt. He only regretted not doing it sooner, because it would have saved him a lot of trouble. As for that business with Lisette, what was done was done. He would have preferred to end things differently with her, but he reminded himself that Lisette she was just another tooth in the cog of war. Just like Rohde himself. Just like everyone.

The hour was later than he had planned, not so much because of the errand involving the *Staber*, but because of the little boy, Leo, who lagged behind at every step. The boy's enthusiasm about going on an adventure was beginning to wane.

"Hurry up, damn you!" he snapped at the boy, his patience

at an end. Everything depended upon their being in position by first light. The boy spoke little German, but Rohde's tone needed no translation.

"I'm hungry," the boy whined in response.

"I told you, do what you are told and you can have something to eat."

The child nodded sullenly.

Already, a red dawn showed to the east, a harbinger of another day of war. And yet the countryside around them remained oblivious. Birds began to sing in the trees. A cow lowed in the distance, signaling that it was ready to be milked.

Rohde looked out across the field, toward the distant hedgerow on the other side. As the light gathered, the details of his killing field became more clear.

Now, he just needed the bait.

To catch a lion ...

"Come here," he said to the boy with a coldness in his voice that made the child give him every bit of his attention. "Put out your hands."

The boy did not understand him, so Rohde roughly grabbed Leo's hands, turned them wrist to wrist, and bound them tightly with a cord he took from his pocket.

The boy winced and whimpered, tried to pull his hands away, but Rohde was having none of that.

He had chosen cord no bigger than a shoelace so that he could bind the boy's wrists tightly with no chance of him wriggling free. Next, he took a rope and tied it around the wrists, where the boy's fingers could never work it free.

He had debated how to go about securing the boy in the field. He had considered, and quickly dismissed, the idea of hamstringing the boy, worried that Leo might die of blood loss before he had served his purpose.

He tugged at the rope. "Come on," he said, half dragging

the boy behind him as he made his way out into the field. The Gewehr 43 was on a sling over his shoulder.

Once they reached roughly the middle of the field, Rohde knotted the free end of the rope around a grazing stake that he had brought for just this purpose. It was a simple metal stake half a meter long, shaped at the end like an upside down stirrup. Using his boot, he stamped the stake deep into the field. Farmers used these stakes to keep grazing horses and cattle in place. He was certain that the stake would be enough to keep the boy just where Rohde wanted him.

Rohde glanced toward the east. The light began to grow much brighter all at once, like the drapes of a darkened room being cast open. The sun was coming up. He had better hurry. Everything depended on him being in position before anyone could see his hiding place.

He could also hear the distant sound of mechanized vehicles from that direction. The Allies were on the move. It would not be long now.

Breathing heavily from the effort of driving home the stake, he knelt beside the boy. Rohde took a chocolate bar from his pocket and presented it to Leo, ruffling his hair as he did so.

"*Au revoir,*" he said, and left him there.

* * *

ROHDE RETURNED to his first hide and settled down to wait. He slid the rifle across the top of the hole. He realized that it would have been better to camouflage the rifle in some way, and silently cursed himself. The light brown wood of the stock seemed to stand out, along with the fact that the finish on the stock was still new and bright. It was too late now to do anything about that.

From his sniper's dugout, he had a clear view across the

field. The boy was just visible through the grass, his head and shoulders making a silhouette against the early morning backdrop of trees and sky and grass.

Using those quiet moments, Rohde took stock of his conscience. He was not so entirely lost that he did not know that his actions could be considered abhorrent. He had whored out the French girl, kidnapped a child to use as bait, and murdered old Hohenfeldt. Shining a light into the corners of his mind, he knew that he should have felt more about that, but any feelings were strangely muted. Perhaps he had been a soldier too long, or perhaps he had allowed his ambition, his burning desire for the Iron Cross, to overshadow everything else. He cast his inner eye one last time on these actions and emotions, then bundled them up and locked them deep within himself.

His opportunity for contemplation did not last long. The early morning peace was broken by an approaching mechanized rumble. Guessing that it must be a Sherman tank, he frowned. He had planned on an assault by men, not machines.

Fortunately for him, the thick boundary of the hedgerow was impregnable to the tank. He could hear it to the west, working its way around the field. The question was, were there any Americans traveling in the tank's wake?

His question was answered when he saw a shadowy figure slip through the tight-knit vegetation on the other side of the field.

The Amis had arrived.

Rohde lined up the post sight on the figure as he emerged. He wished that he'd had time to at least make a few test shots of the Gewehr. On the job training. That was the Wehrmacht for you. What else was new?

The *Staber* had said that it was sighted in for 200 meters, so Rohde could accept that as fact. Hohenfeldt had been a bastard, but he was exacting about the details of weapons.

Rohde had paced off the field, so he knew that where he had placed the boy was at the 200-meter mark. The far edge of the field was twice that distance.

The American soldier entered Rohde's field of view within the rifle scope.

He held his breath.

Although the telescopic sight was adjustable, all of the scopes used by the sniper were famously finicky. He could change the elevation with a few clicks, but there was no certainty that the scope would return to its current sighted-in range with any accuracy.

Instead, it made more sense to raise his aim. Normally, he aimed for the belt buckle. Now, he aimed a little higher. Complete accuracy did not matter so much; hitting a man anywhere from the chest to the groin would put him down. A man made a long target, up and down; it was mainly the windage—from side to side—that proved more challenging. That would not be much of a factor in the still morning air.

Although a bullet was a vast technological improvement over a stone or a spear, the same rules of gravity applied to the modern warrior. Any projectile was pulled down by the force of gravity, whether it was a spear or a bullet. To throw a spear any distance, one had to throw it high. The same principle applied to a bullet. Fire it along a curved trajectory, and it would travel farther before gravity worked its inexorable pull upon it.

Rohde aimed high, and fired.

Instantly, he experienced two pleasant surprises. First, the bullet struck the GI dead center and sent him spinning into the field. Second, the recoil of the Gewehr 43 was much lighter due to the operation of the semi-automatic rifle's gas recoil system.

There was no working the bolt and slapping it back into place, forcing him to readjust his aim in the process. Instead, the new rifle spat out the brass casing and loaded a fresh round instantly.

For good measure, Rohde shot the GI again.

Out in the field, the boy was frightened by the sound of the shots as well as the bloodshed he had just witnessed.

Leo began to scream.

The boy's cries worked to perfection. Almost instantly, another American appeared, and then another. Having just seen one of their comrades shot, it was likely that they would have kept their heads down if it hadn't been for the boy's screams.

Rohde fired once, twice. Two more GIs collapsed into the field. The first one lay still, killed instantly, but the second was on his elbows, trying futilely to drag himself to safety. His own pitiful cries joined those of the boy.

The devil himself could not have orchestrated a more horrible symphony.

Rohde chided himself for not thinking of shooting to wound, rather than to kill. He had been too excited about the new rifle to think clearly. At least some of the time, he realized that missing had its own rewards.

Despite the noise, the GIs were not so eager to take any action with a German sniper in play. A few shots began to zip across the field, but the bullets came nowhere near Rohde's hiding place. He guessed that there were at least a dozen GIs hidden at the edge of the field. If the GIs had opened up on him, or if they had used a machine gun, he might have been in trouble with a swarm of bullets coming at him, hiding place or not. But Rohde guessed that the GIs were afraid of hitting the boy.

That was the trouble with Americans, he thought. They were too soft-hearted. If it hadn't been for the sheer advantage of numbers and air power, they would not be winning this war.

He could see a couple of puffs or flashes where the GIs were shooting from cover. Rohde fired at those spots and the guns fell silent. After that, the return fire was only sporadic.

The cries of the wounded GI and of the boy seemed to grow louder.

Rohde let the earth hug his belly, and he settled down to wait for whatever target showed itself next.

CHAPTER TWENTY-FIVE

HIGH ABOVE THE FRENCH COUNTRYSIDE, a raven soared on outstretched wings, surveying the landscape.

Since ancient times, ravens had gathered in the skies above the battlefields of Europe. They were scavengers by nature, and instinct had long since taught them that where men clashed with weapons, the ravens would find rich rewards.

What seemed so gruesome to the survivors of battle was simply natural instinct to a raven.

If someone could have seen the French countryside with a raven's eye and cleared away all of the trees and hedgerows, all of the tall summer grass and stone walls, then the scene might resemble one of those miniature villages and landscapes in a train garden that sometimes appeared during the holidays.

But this was no peaceful holiday scene. In August 1944, the French countryside was a tableau of violence.

First, the eye would be captured by entire units on the move. It was rather an awesome sight. Masses of American troops crept forward, tiny figures in olive drab, while in the distance were English, Canadian, and even Polish troops.

Blue-gray uniforms on the tableau showed the German forces, forming well-demarcated defensive lines. Here and there, pockets of soldiers in olive drab and blue-gray uniforms faced each other across fields and woodlands.

These forces included the British 2nd Army, Canadian 1st Army, Polish troops, and the German 7th Army and 5th Panzer Division.

By early August, the Germans were boxed into an area 20 miles long and five miles deep. Allied forces were squeezing in on them from three sides. This was the beginning of what would come to be known as the Falaise Gap or Pocket. The French and British pronounced it as *poh-ket*.

Not particularly notable for any strategic value, it was simply one of those turns of fate that all these troops seemed fated to clash here at Falaise and Argentan. This was where the German 7th Army had found itself herded by circumstance as Allied forces pushed in. Like water finding its level, the German troops had filed into a wide valley ringed by low hills. The Allies wasted no time getting artillery position on those hills, and then opened fire.

It was not unlike the situation that had brought Union and Confederate troops to clash at the town of Gettysburg in the Pennsylvania countryside eighty years before. No one had set out to fight a battle there. The names of commanders then had been Lee and Longstreet and Meade. Now it was Patton and Von Kluge and Montgomery.

Not even the Germans were sure how many troops were caught in this gap, but it was anywhere from 80,000 to 100,000 men—a vast number of German soldiers whose destruction seemed near.

On August 12, however, General Omar Bradley ordered Patton to halt his steamrolling advance. His 3rd Army had been surging across France, sometimes moving faster than the Germans could retreat. At these orders, Patton was almost apoplectic, considering that the total annihilation of German forces seemed within his grasp.

At least, that was how Patton saw it. Bradley's view was that Patton's lines were stretched too thin as it was, to the point that the Germans might break through, with disastrous results. In typical Bradley fashion, he later explained that he'd rather have Patton offer a strong shoulder to prop up the Allied advance than to suffer a broken neck.

Having been on Ike's naughty list for most of the previous year, Patton decided to obey orders. With the advance stopped, it left a gap just two miles wide in the Allied lines. Still, thousands of German troops managed to escape toward Germany through that gap.

The noose around German forces at Falaise and Argentan kept tightening.

The Germans were not helped by the fact that their commander, Von Kluge, had been ordered back to Germany on August 18. He was a suspected conspirator in the attempt on Hitler's life. Rather than face punishment, he committed suicide by swallowing cyanide.

Walter Modell replaced Von Kluge. Though late to the game, Modell was an adept and capable general. He threw himself into the chaos of this last stand, hoping to keep much of the army intact to fight another day, in Germany itself.

If the raven overhead had good weather for flying, so did the Allied planes.

The weather in early August was all blue skies and sunshine, made to order for air operations. The Luftwaffe was virtually gone, either destroyed on the ground in Operation Cobra and subsequent bombing, or simply overwhelmed by the sheer number of Allied fighters. The German airmen were mostly inexperienced and poorly trained at this point.

Goring had proven to be a poor choice to head up the Luftwaffe throughout the war. One could only imagine the different outcome of the air war if an Admiral Donitz had been in charge. Unlike the Luftwaffe, the Kriegsmarine remained a dangerous adversary.

The British Hawker Typhoons and P-47 Thunderbolts flew their sorties, mostly unchallenged, unleashing their bombs, rockets, and machine guns on German targets. And it was a target-rich environment, with trains, tanks, and convoys ripe for the taking.

Despite the Allied planes, German tanks roamed the tableau like iron wolves, looking to pick off prey.

All in all, it was battle on a massive, sprawling scale. The movement of men and machines appeared impersonal and remote. But each of those tiny figures below represented a life filled with hopes and desires and fears. The cold eye of the raven was indifferent to their fates.

Here and there stood a quiet stone farmhouse, surrounded on all sides by troops and tanks. Seeing the violence to come, one hoped that the occupants had fled.

One such farmstead was Lisette's. This morning, the raven's eye would have picked out the figure of Lisette, running frantically from the house to the barn to the fields, searching for her nephew, who was nowhere to be found.

If the raven squinted, he might even have seen the small figures of American soldiers moving across the landscape, toward a skirmish being fought across a small field not far from Argentan.

Far below, one of those snipers looked up, put his rifle to his shoulder, and shot the raven from the sky.

CHAPTER TWENTY-SIX

"SHOW OFF," Vaccaro said. "Nobody else I know can hit a bird flying."

"I don't much like ravens," Cole responded. "Devil birds, if you ask me. Shot that one through the eye."

Vaccaro snorted.

Cole moved down the dirt road, eyes scanning to the horizon. Maybe Vaccaro was right and shooting the bird was showing off, but he'd had an itchy trigger finger all morning. Short of any available Germans, he'd had to shoot *something*, goddammit.

The morning light was still growing, promising more sunny weather. After the clouds and gloom of early summer, this was a welcome change. It was as if the sun knew that there was a war going on, and showed its disapproval by withholding its warmth. He had longed for a single summer day from back home, with the sky bright blue against the mountains and a warm breeze scented with woods and wildflowers.

They had started off crossing grass, leaving their boots wet with dew, and now the dust from the road clung to them. He remembered all that spit and polish bullshit from boot camp. Cole hadn't seen the point. Hell, he was just glad to have boots. There had been plenty of times, as a boy, when he'd simply gone barefoot.

With growing wariness, he saw the countryside close in around them as they walked. For a mountain boy, it was a claustrophobic feeling. The countryside here was too flat. Cole longed for a hill to climb so that he could get the lay of the land. So far, he was not enamored of France. He thought that the whole landscape looked too tame from centuries of farming.

The day promised to be a sunny one, enabling the flyboys to do their job. With the planes flying sorties overhead, the German Panzers would be run to ground.

Cole himself felt edgy. Like something was about to happen. He had learned to trust that instinct. It had kept him alive so far.

Their orders were simple. He and Vaccaro were assigned to counter sniper measures. As they moved toward Falaise, there seemed to be no shortage of enemy snipers.

Cole hoped to meet one sniper in particular. When he thought about it, maybe *hoped* wasn't the right word. He itched to put a bullet in that sniper.

He looked up for another bird to shoot, but the sky was empty.

This morning, they had taken along a kid named Harper to serve as a spotter. More than two months after D-Day, fresh troops like Harper were being rotated into combat units. Rumor had it that Harper had been in the typing pool and asked for a transfer to the field. That either made him brave, or awfully stupid.

Harper had claimed to have some skill with a rifle, so Lieutenant Mulholland had gotten the bright idea to send the kid along with Cole and Vaccaro this morning.

"Maybe you can teach him a thing or two," Mulholland had said.

"We don't need no help, lieutenant," Cole said.

The lieutenant had shot him a look. "It's not a suggestion, Cole. It's an order."

"Yes, sir," Cole said through gritted teeth. Lately, there had been a lot of tension between Cole and Mulholland. It didn't take a genius figure out that it was over that French girl, Jolie Molyneux.

There wasn't an extra sniper rifle, so Harper carried an M1 with open sights. So far, nobody had figured out how to put a scope on one of those, which was a shame, because a semi-automatic sniper rifle wasn't a bad idea.

Unlike the Germans or the Russians or even the English, the United States Army did not have an official sniper school. Soldiers with an aptitude as marksmen were simply given a scoped rifle and on-the-job training.

"Got any advice?" Harper had asked as they moved out.

"Yeah," Vaccaro said. "Don't get shot."

Cole looked Harper up and down with those weird eyes of his, but said nothing.

Now, Harper hung back and walked for a while with Vaccaro, letting Cole take point.

Every now and then, Harper glanced almost furtively at the sniper. Cole made him nervous. The U.S. Army wanted every soldier to see himself as lean, mean, fighting machine, but there was a fine line between being a soldier and being a killer. Whatever that special something was that made someone a killer, Cole radiated it like an Old West gunfighter.

"What's with him, anyway?" Harper asked Vaccaro.

"Just leave him alone and stay out of his way," Vaccaro said quietly. "He's in one of his moods."

"What mood is that?"

"The kind where he wants to shoot something. You wanna volunteer?"

"No thanks."

"You see, kid, Cole's got himself a feud going with that German sniper who shot him up. He's a hillbilly, so he's never happier than when he has a feud going. This is real Hatfield and McCoy stuff."

"The one I feel sorry for is the German, because he doesn't know yet that Cole is out to get him."

Harper gestured at the woods and fields surrounding them. "And just how are they going to find each other?"

"You ever been at a USO dance and run into a guy from the same high school?"

"Yeah, something like that."

"Thousands of guys on the other side of the ocean, and you run into one you know. What are the odds, right? It's a small world, kid. It's even smaller when Cole is looking for you."

They walked on. In the distance, they could hear shooting and the dull *thud* of artillery that meant somebody was catching hell. So far, it was quiet in their neck of the woods.

They passed a body lying in a ditch. It was a dead American.

"Goddamn Krauts," Cole said bitterly, looking at the body. He spat.

Harper and Vaccaro hung back a little farther.

The sound of gunfire erupted not that far ahead of them. Bursts of fire, followed by solitary rifle shots. It sounded like a lopsided fight. But if there was a sniper involved, those solitary rifle shots might be devastating.

A few minutes later, a soldier came trotting up the road.

"Hey!" he shouted when he caught sight of Cole. He ran up to them, nearly breathless. He took a good look at Cole's rifle. "Is that a sniper rifle?"

Cole could see that the soldier had been running, and he looked a little scared, so he gave him the benefit of the doubt. "Well, it ain't a banjo."

"Good." The soldier was too rattled to be anything but serious. "The lieutenant back there sent me to find you. He said to look for somebody named Cole." He waved his arm in the general direction of the road behind him. "Is that you?"

"That'd be me."

Vaccaro spoke up. "He asked for you by name? What the hell?"

"Shut up, Vaccaro." Cole looked at the runner. "I reckon I'm Cole. So what's the situation?" He pronounced it, *sitch-ee-ay-shun*.

"A sniper has us pinned down. And if that's not bad enough, the sniper has got a kid tied up in the field. He's using him as goddamn bait. A couple of our guys got greased trying to rescue him." He gulped. "It's awful."

"Let me take my banjo here, and go have a look."

* * *

THEY SET off down the road at a trot. Cole moved with a graceful lope that was hard for the others to keep up with.

Still, Vaccaro managed to pant a question at the soldier who had found them on the road. "Are you sure the lieutenant didn't mention me? Vaccaro?"

"I'm pretty sure he didn't."

Cole looked back over his shoulder. "Hey, quit jabberin' and keep up."

He picked up the pace. They could tell that they were getting close by the louder sound of gunfire.

The soldier stopped running near a gap in the hedge. The sound of firing was very close now. "This is where I cut through."

Cole didn't know what he was walking into, but he knew it wouldn't be good. If this soldier was right, and the German sniper had tied some kid up in the field as bait, it meant that the German had set a trap and that he had every advantage.

What kind of German sniper would do that? Cole suspected that it might very well be the one who had ambushed him.

Cole hesitated before plunging down the path. He didn't like this set up one bit. Like the soldiers in the squad that was now pinned down, he would just be walking into the sniper's trap.

It didn't help that he was ringed in on every side by trees, hedges, and flat fields. His ears were telling him more than his eyes. But he couldn't shoot with his ears. What he needed to do was get up high and get the lay of the land.

He thought about the church they had seen in the distance. It wasn't exactly a cathedral, but the steeple was at least a couple of stories tall, and the church itself had been built on high ground. It was likely that the church was far beyond rifle range from this field, but at least he could see what was going on, and then make his move from there.

He turned back the way they had come and started running.

"Cole?" Vaccaro shouted after him. "What the hell?"

"Come on," Cole called, and without further explanation, he ran back toward where he had seen that church steeple.

CHAPTER TWENTY-SEVEN

THE CHURCH WAS of modest dimensions, no more than thirty-five feet long and maybe twenty-five feet across. More of a chapel, in actuality, than a church, and the building definitely was not going to be confused with a cathedral. A plaque identified it as Église St. Dominic. It was built of huge stone block, hauled from God knows where, with each massive block weighing hundreds of pounds. One thing about these French, Cole thought, was that they built to last. If only they had taken the same care to defend the very existence of their country.

Once he had left the road, Cole approached cautiously. The church looked deserted, but with the territory surrounding them in flux, he didn't want to walk up on any German patrols. That would ruin his day in a hurry.

He pressed himself against the right front corner of the church and listened. Didn't hear anything inside.

Cole looked behind him and gave the hand signal for the others to approach. They did so, running toward the church in a crouch. He noticed that Vaccaro kept his eyes on the steeple, with his rifle pointed in that direction. The city boy was learning.

Vaccaro ran up, panting, an exasperated expression on his face. Harper ran up next. The other soldier had returned to his squad.

"You don't have to fight the war alone, you know," Vaccaro said. "You could tell me what the hell you're up to."

"I'm gonna tell you now," Cole said. "What I want to do is get up in that steeple, and see if I can get a look at where this sniper is dug in."

Vaccaro turned to Harper. "Kid, you stay down here and keep watch. Keep a sharp eye out. I sure as hell don't want to get trapped in that church if a German patrol comes along."

Harper nodded, and instantly turned his eyes toward the landscape surrounding the church.

The church was not locked. Cole pushed the massive wooden door open with his shoulder, did a quick check inside, and then stepped all the way in with Vaccaro behind him.

Inside, the church smelled of dampness and incense. This was an old peasant church so there were no pews, but only bare flagstones and a simply carved altar flanked by simple stained glass windows whose light barely penetrated the gloom.

Nor were there any steps leading to the steeple. Instead, there was only a ladder.

Briefly, Cole thought about Von Stenger, who had used a tunnel to get into a church inside Bienville and then began shooting up the town's defenders like a fox inside a henhouse. That Von Stenger had been a slippery son of a bitch.

Cole went up the ladder first, followed by Vaccaro.

"Do you think Harper is going to be OK watching our six?"

"Once we get up in that steeple, we ought to see anyone coming at us from a long ways off."

They emerged through a trapdoor into the church steeple itself. It was no more than six feet on a side, hemmed in by low stone walls topped by a wooden rail so rotten that it would be hazardous to lean against, all covered by a slate-shingled hip roof. The floor was chalky white with pigeon droppings. There was a bell rope, but no bell. Cole suspected that the Germans had taken it away and melted it down, which was a common practice of the occupiers.

From the steeple, there was a good view of the surrounding countryside. The old church had been built at a kind of crossroads, and four dirt roads led away from the chapel. In the distance, they could see the field where the fight was taking place.

HIDDEN IN THE FIELD, Rohde had to wait longer than expected for the Americans to get up their nerve again. The sun climbed higher and began to beat down mercilessly on the wounded.

The boy had mostly fallen silent and was sitting down now, but the wounded GI was still calling out, this time for water.

He saw a flicker of movement through the trees. The Americans were trying once more to break through and get across the field. This time they tried a simple diversion. Two men ran forward, firing from the hip, while another man far to their left ran in a crouch toward the boy.

Their ploy was simple enough. They hoped to keep the sniper's attention focused on the two men who were firing while the third man reached the boy undetected in order to free him.

But Rohde was having none of that.

"Look at them, Carl," he spoke aloud to his dead brother. "They must think that I am a fool."

The new rifle made it easy. He fixed the sight on the man trying to rescue Leo and took him out. Then he swung the rifle toward the two men and put them down with two quick shots.

Finally, one of the other Americans couldn't stand the pitiful cries any longer and broke cover, carrying a canteen.

This soldier zigzagged as he ran, which made him a difficult target. He was carrying only a canteen, and had stripped off his gear and even his helmet in an effort to be more fleet of foot.

And could this one run like a rabbit! Rohde fired, his bullet singing through the air where the GI had been only a moment before. Rohde fired two more rapid shots, pulling the trigger, *tap*, *tap*. The runner went down.

After that flurry of activity, all was quiet for several minutes. The only sound came from the boy still tied up in the field. Leo was whimpering like a frightened puppy.

* * *

COLE WATCHED it all through the scope. It was a goddamn slaughter. He itched to get a shot at the German sniper. If nothing else, maybe he could rattle him enough to lay off the trigger.

With that thought in mind, he tugged the Confederate flag from a pocket. It was the same flag that old man Hollis had wrapped his knife in. Not knowing what else to do with it at the time, Cole had stuffed it in a pocket. Now he knew.

He took the knife and used it to secure the flag to the wooden rail in the steeple so that it hung down, clearly visible from a long way off. He reckoned it would be like waving a red flag at a bull. Just fine with him. Although marking his location with a bright Confederate flag went against any lick of sense, he thought that maybe he could goad that sniper into doing something stupid.

He set the rifle across the low stone wall of the steeple, then put his eye to the scope.

Still nothing.

* * *

COLE TOOK the binoculars from Vaccaro and glassed the field. He could see bodies in the grass, and a child doubled over in the middle of the field, covering his head with his arms. Poor kid, Cole thought. Bullets must be flying around him, and yet he hadn't moved.

Then, through the binoculars, Cole saw the reason why. With a shock, he realized that a rope ran from the boy's waist to a stake in the ground.

Staked out like a goat.

What sort of sick son of a bitch would do that to a kid? *The German sniper. Rohde.* Cole felt his blood begin to boil.

"Any idea where the sniper's at?" Vaccaro asked in a whisper, as if the German might hear him.

"Not yet," Cole said. He handed back the binoculars. "You take a look."

Cole judged the distance to be nearly 1,000 yards. More than half a mile. A long way to shoot. One hell of a long way, as a matter of fact.

Some things were in his favor. There wasn't so much as a breath of wind. He knew his rifle intimately and could coax every last yard out of it.

The distance seemed even farther in the reduced amplification of the rifle scope.

"Vaccaro, I want you to keep those binoculars glued to

that field. You see so much as a whisker of that son of a bitch, you let me know."

"Got it."

The fact that Vaccaro had not said anything previously spoke volumes. His silence indicated that he thought Cole must have gone crazy to think that he could hit anything that far away.

Cole agreed, but short of picking up the church and moving it, this was the best vantage point he was going to find.

Cole could see the boy in the field. The binoculars were stronger, so through the scope he could no longer see the rope, but he could imagine where it was, stretched taught about a foot above the ground.

Keeping that picture in his mind, he aimed and fired.

* * *

ROHDE WATCHED AND WAITED. The situation in the field had fallen into a silent stalemate that was broken by a distant rifle report.

Moving at supersonic speed, the bullet cracked across the open expanse of the field somewhere in Leo's vicinity.

Another shot kicked up the dirt near Leo's feet.

Rohde wondered who was shooting, and what the shooter was trying to hit.

There came a third shot. Again, it kicked up dirt at the boy's feet.

* * *

"WHAT THE HELL, Cole? Are you trying to kill that kid?" Through the binoculars, Vaccaro had seen the dirt erupt where the bullet struck.

"Where did I hit?"

"Four o'clock and five feet short of the boy," Vaccaro said in a strained voice.

Cole worked the bolt. Fired.

"What the hell are you doing? You're gonna kill that kid."

"High or low?" Cole asked.

"Neither," Vaccaro said. "That bullet hit at three o'clock about two feet from the kid. Jesus, Cole. What the hell are you doing? Don't shoot that kid."

In his mind's eye, Cole kept the sight picture of where the crosshairs had been for the last shot. He imagined just where a taut rope would be, running from the boy to a stake in the ground.

This wasn't aiming. This wasn't even hoping. This was more like a daydream of a shot.

CHAPTER TWENTY-EIGHT

COLE TOOK A BREATH. He could not see the rope securing the boy, but he could imagine it there. He let his finger put tension on the trigger.

Traveling at 2700 feet per second over a distance that would take a man 15 minutes to walk across, the bullet cut the taut rope like a knife.

Through the scope, he saw the boy jump up and run.

* * *

ROHDE WATCHED in amazement as Leo ran like the wind, right toward the arms of an American GI who had materialized out of the woods and stood there waiting for the boy.

Rohde stared in disbelief before it dawned on him that the shot he had just heard had not been random at all. It was intended to cut the rope keeping Leo tethered to the stake. Who could possibly make such a shot? And from how far out?

He raised his rifle. Instantly, the post sight settled on the boy. He started to squeeze the trigger.

* * *

"COLE! I saw the son of a bitch," Vaccaro said.

"Tell me where he's at."

"I don't—hold on, hold on. There's a kind of ditch down there if you look real hard. It's in front of that clump of bushes."

Cole screwed his eye tighter to the telescope. "Yeah, I see it now. I don't see *him*, but I see where the field's been dug up."

It was a long way to shoot, but Cole's bullet hit close. It would be enough to rattle Rohde.

* * *

A BULLET ZIPPED past Rohde's ear, causing him to flinch just at the moment that his own rifle fired. *Damn, but that was close!*

An involuntary shiver ran through him, as if the bullet had set off shock waves in the air. He glimpsed the boy being caught up in the arms of the American on the other side of the field, and both of them scurried to safety.

Rohde kept very still, waiting for another bullet. There was just one shot. That was the trademark of a sniper. Hugging his belly to the dirt of the trench, Rohde considered that he'd heard only the distant report of a rifle. Whoever had fired that bullet was very far away. Could it possibly be the American hillbilly sniper whom Rohde had hoped to lure with his trap? There was no telling without catching a glimpse of that helmet with its Confederate flag.

If it *was* the American sniper, he was a damn good shot.

His heart hammering, Rohde began to wonder if he'd gotten more than he had bargained for. He had imagined himself having the upper hand, but not the other way around.

There was no going back now. He must use his wits to survive this, and to shoot the American hillbilly in the bargain.

Instantly, Rohde made up his mind. He could have shot at the retreating GIs, but the American sniper had somehow spotted him. His first sniper's nest was compromised.

Betting that all eyes were on the GIs trying to get to safety, Rohde used the shallow ditch he had cut to wriggle backward out of his hidey hole. The ditch led to the sort of hunter's blind he had created 20 feet away. With any luck, the American sniper would make some misstep, and Rohde would pluck him off from the safety of his second hide.

He rolled out of the ditch and slipped behind the screen of multiflora rose and brush. He kept his movements to a minimum, trying not to attract any attention. He paused, holding his breath, but no one was shooting at him.

The only thing that he didn't like about this second hide was that it provided concealment, rather than cover. This was a fundamental from sniper school. Concealment kept one hidden. It was like standing behind a curtain. Cover actually stopped bullets. It was like standing behind a brick wall. The hole in the ground had provided both, and he had been able to fire from the position as well. The hunter's blind that he had made offered concealment alone. Clumps of bushes were not going to stop a bullet.

* * *

"THERE HE IS AGAIN! He's back in that bush."

"That wild rose bush?"

"Do I look like a goddamn gardener to you?"

"All right, now there's lots of bushes in that field. Is it that bush with them little white flowers on it?"

"Yeah, yeah, that's the one. Dead center of that bush, about three feet up, not down on the ground."

Cole fired again.

* * *

SOMEHOW, the American had spotted him.

One moment, Rohde had considered himself safe, and the next, a bullet seemed to reach out of the air and grab at his uniform jacket, plucking at the fabric. He cursed again. This sniper must have eyes like an eagle!

With a final burst of speed, Rohde ran and pitched forward into the hedgerow itself, burrowing deep within until he reached the rocky shelf that he had cleared.

Heart pounding, he threw himself down on his belly, got his elbows under him, and began scanning the far edge of the field for any sign of the sniper.

But those shots had sounded so far away. It didn't make sense. He played his scope even farther out, looking for a tree or hillock that could have provided a vantage point for the enemy sniper.

Where, where, where—

He scanned a few trees, and just as quickly dismissed them.

With the scope, his field of view wandered even farther out. Finally, he focused on a church steeple on a slight rise far beyond the field. He recognized the church as Église St. Domini, which he had passed often enough in his *Jäger* missions.

The church presided over a village crossroads, appearing as ancient and neglected as the last apple on the tree after the frost. The church was high enough to have a commanding view of the field, although at that distance, any men in the field would appear to be hardly bigger than ants. As the Americans measured it, the distance would be 1000 yards.

Realization slowly dawned on Rohde that the American sniper must be in that church steeple. There was no other possibility.

Several thoughts ran through his mind. First of all, he was shocked that any man could shoot that far with any accuracy in combat conditions. At that distance, a shooter would need the eyesight of an eagle, with nerves as steady as a marble statue.

While Rohde felt reasonably confident about shots at 400 meters, anything much beyond that was like whistling in the wind. And yet, Rohde was himself an impressive marksman.

A tremor of fear and awe ran through him. Could it be the hillbilly sniper? No one was that good with a rifle.

His own scope was not strong enough to pick out any details of the church, so he reached for the Zeiss binoculars in his pack. They were far larger and more precise.

At that distance, he thought, the sniper must surely have a spotter who had a strong pair of binoculars to help the shooter pick out targets.

He put down the rifle and trained the binoculars on the church.

Built of squat blocks of stone, the ivy-covered walls made it appear as if the old church had grown out of the country-side itself. The steeple was far from grand, crowning the church more like a squat bowler hat than a top hat.

He did not know what he expected to see, but it was not *this*. What sprang to his eye was a small flag like those that children waved along parade routes. It fluttered from one window of the steeple. This flag clearly displayed the Stars and Bars that Major Dorfmann had described. The rebel flag of the Confederacy.

It was clear that the flag was displayed as a calling card. It was as good as a sign announcing that the American hillbilly sniper had set up shop there.

Rohde fired at the church, although he didn't have any real target. All discipline was gone. He was shooting out of anger and frustration. Breaking every rule in his sniper's textbook. But damn it all, it felt good.

* * *

A BULLET SLAPPED at the stone walls of the church and whipsawed away, the noise of the ricochet sending a twang down Cole's spine.

Another bullet struck the church, another smacked the steeple. So, the German had spotted the flag. Just as Cole had hoped, he was charging like a bull, shooting in a hurry, not aiming at any definite target except the church itself.

"Not a lot of cover up here," Vaccaro said nervously.

"He ain't gonna hit shit."

At this range, Cole was damn near shooting blind. He took his best guess at where the German sniper lay hidden, and squeezed off another round.

* * *

SEVERAL BULLETS CLIPPED the brush near Rohde's hiding place, but he managed to ignore them. The sniper was only estimating his location. One shot came very close, the bullet striking the old twisted tree limb overhead. Rohde kept his eyes pressed to the rifle scope. Finally, it was the sound of machine-gun fire that caused him to wrest his attention away. On the other side of the field, the squad of Americans was advancing. They kept up a steady fire.

Time to go.

* * *

"HE'S RUNNING! I saw something move through the bushes."

"Watch him, now. Where's he at?"

"Back in the hedgerow. Two o'clock from your goddamn rose bush."

Short of putting himself in Vaccaro's head, Cole had to rely on his spotter's description. He fired. Worked the bolt. Fired again. Now he was just guessing, shooting in the German's general direction. Making the German keep his head down.

The firing at the church stopped.

* * *

"DID YOU GET HIM?" Vaccaro's voice was pitched high with excitement.

Cole didn't know. *Had* he got the German? There was no way to tell for sure, short of working their way over there. But something hadn't felt right. He couldn't have explained it to anyone else, not even to Vaccaro, but he *knew* when he hit a target. Cole was fairly certain that the sniper had simply melted away.

"Didn't get him yet." Cole spat on the stone floor and lowered the rifle. "That would just be too damn easy, wouldn't it?"

CHAPTER TWENTY-NINE

COLE AND VACCARO sat up in the steeple, both of them smoking cigarettes and letting the adrenaline ebb out of their systems. From this high up, they had a good view of the surrounding countryside. Still, they kept their heads down. Cole stuffed the Confederate flag back into his pocket. He had sent his message to the sniper; no point in attracting additional attention.

With the German sniper gone, the American GIs were no longer pinned down in the field and had moved on. Across the countryside, Allied troops were moving toward Argentan and Falaise as if part of a huge incoming flood tide. The squad was one small eddy in that flood.

Some soldiers from the squad would not be going anywhere, however. Their bodies lay under the gray sky, victims of the German sniper. A few days from now, thousands of miles away, telegrams would be delivered to the doors of the dead soldiers' parents or wives.

Cole decided that maybe it was the German whose bullets had traveled the farthest today.

"Hell of a shot, Hillbilly," Vaccaro said, as if reading his thoughts. "You saved that kid and sent that Kraut sniper running for cover."

"Even a blind squirrel finds a nut now and then."

"And a stopped clock is right twice a day, too." Vaccaro shook his head and grinned. "See? Your hillbilly sayings are rubbing off on me. Now, let's get the hell out of here."

The German sniper had melted away into the landscape. They had seen the boy running for the American lines. With any luck, he was back at the command post right about now, eating a chocolate bar.

They went back down the ladder into the stillness of the old chapel. Cole liked to hear a good preacher thump a Bible now and then, but back home that had mostly been at clapboard-sided country churches and camp meetings, out in the open. This stone church felt too dark and brooding. The God who dwelt here wasn't like the one back home.

Harper looked shook up. He had been transferred from the typing pool just a few days before, after all. "Did you hear those bullets hit the church? God, what a sound a ricochet makes."

"I guess it's a little louder than that bell on the typewriter when you get to the end of a line," Vaccaro said with a smirk.

Cole touched his shoulder. "You did good, Harper. I been gettin' shot at for months now, and I still ain't used to it."

* * *

THE FORWARD COMMAND post consisted of a barnyard where a Jeep was parked, a map spread across its still-ticking hood. The air smelled unpleasantly of fresh manure churned up by the Jeep's tires. Three officers huddled over the map, one of them being Lieutenant Mulholland. He looked up eagerly as Cole, Vaccaro, and Harper walked in.

"Did you get that son of a bitch?" Mulholland asked.

Cole shook his head. "No, but he run off with his tail between his legs."

"I guess that's something. These goddamn Kraut snipers are wreaking havoc with the advance, and that sniper Rohde is the worst of them," Mulholland said. He turned to the map and thumped it with the flat of his hand for emphasis. "We've got an opportunity here to bag the whole German army, or what's left of it, anyway. There's a Polish division to the northeast, moving in to help us out."

"Polish?" They had seen their share of Brits and Canadians in Normandy, but Polish troops were something new.

"Yeah, so try not to shoot any of them by accident, and let's hope to hell they don't shoot us."

One of the other officers took his eyes off the map and looked at Cole. It was a captain whom Cole did not recognize.

"You must be Cole," he said. "I could tell by that 'Stars and Bars' on your helmet. I read about you in that newspaper article by Ernie Pyle."

Nearby, Vaccaro muttered, "Jesus, did anyone *not* read that story? Other than the hillbilly, I mean."

The captain went on, "That was a helluva good story. I did want to know though, what kind of name Micajah was? Never heard that one before."

"Micajah was a prophet in the Bible, sir."

"Is that so? The lieutenant here says you can shoot the buttons off a German at four hundred yards."

Cole was more than a little surprised that Mulholland would brag about him. Whatever animosity remained toward Cole over Jolie Molyneux must be wearing off.

Cole drawled, "If I get a German in my sights, sir, I'll be sure to shoot off more than his buttons."

The captain laughed. "I'll bet you will. Give 'em hell, soldier."

"Yes, sir."

"And get some rest, boys. All of you. This whole damn countryside is about to become a battlefield. What's left of the German army is over there." The captain waved vaguely to the east. "We've got the Brits closing in from the north, the Polish coming at them from the south, and none other than General Patton himself going straight into their teeth. With any luck, we'll finish the war right here and be home for Christmas. It's up to us, boys."

Cole distrusted enthusiastic officers. He moved off, intending to fill his canteen. It was already past mid-day, and humid.

Mulholland caught up with him. "Listen, Cole. We may have some intel on this German sniper, Rohde."

"Yeah?"

"You know that little French kid that Rohde tied up in the field? Rohde kidnapped the boy and used him as bait. Talk about a heartless bastard. The kid's aunt turned up to claim him. Some of our guys found her walking along the road and drove her here. The boy's father is here too. The man claims to be in the French Resistance, by the way."

Cole snorted. "Now that we just about won the war for them, half the men in France are claiming to be in the Resistance."

"Don't be too hard on them, Cole. Don't forget that without the French, we wouldn't have won the Revolutionary War."

Cole snorted at that. "My great great granddaddy fought the British. He picked off more than a few Redcoats with his flintlock rifle. I reckon *that's* what helped win the Revolution more than these Frenchies, judging from what I seen so far."

Mulholland looked sideways at Cole. He thought it was easy enough to picture Cole himself in buckskins and a coonskin cap. "With all respect to your great great grandaddy, now it's our turn to return the favor to the French people."

"If you say so."

"This isn't the 18th century, Cole. It's tough to fight the Germans with a few old hunting rifles and shotguns."

Cole wasn't so sure about that. He tried to imagine how things would have turned out for the Germans if they invaded the mountain country back home.

"I reckon," he said noncommittally.

"Anyhow, the boy's aunt" —Mulholland pronounced it *awnt*, while in Cole's mind it was *ant*— "knew this Rohde well. Real well, if you know what I mean."

"What you're sayin' is that she's a collaborator?" Cole spat, adding in a minuscule way to the barnyard mud.

"It looks that way, and her brother—the boy's father— isn't real happy about that, I can tell you. Be that as it may, she could have useful information to help us nail this Rohde."

Cole looked around. The barnyard teamed with exhausted GIs. In the shadow of the barn, he could see a boy and a young woman, who was engaged in a heated argument with a Frenchman in his late twenties. Judging by the man's rugged clothes, and the rifle slung over his shoulder, Cole decided that this must be the Resistance fighter.

He and Mulholland walked over. The girl looked up at their approach. Cole noted the pretty, round face, with greenish eyes surrounded by dark curls. She wore an old dress that was worn thin and that clutched tightly across her hips, accentuating her figure. If Rohde had been collaborating with that body, he was one lucky son of a bitch.

Beside him, Cole also sensed Mulholland giving the girl a furtive going over. *Damn*, he thought. *The last thing I need is me and Mulholland barking up the same tree again.* The tree in this case being an attractive French girl in a tight dress.

"*Excusez moi, mademoiselle,*" Mulholland began, using his

stilted college French. "*Nous voulons savoir sur le tireur d'élite. Celui nommé Rohde.*" *We want to know about the sniper. The one named Rohde.*

At the mention of the sniper's name, the Frenchman launched a fresh tirade at his sister. Cole didn't know any French, but when he heard the brother practically spit the word *putain* at her, Cole was fairly certain that the Frenchman had called his sister a whore.

Then the Frenchman stepped forward and slapped her.

The sight of his angry red hand print on her pretty face was nearly too much to bear. The girl might be a collaborator, but she also looked tired and frightened. When the Frenchman drew back his hand to hit her again, Mulholland raised his hand like he was asking a question and said in his sternest Sunday School teacher voice, "Now, now."

Cole slid between the girl and her brother, blocking him from hitting her again. When he tried to get around Cole, Cole moved with him.

The Frenchman was a farmer by trade, heavy through the shoulders from farm work, and if he couldn't hit his sister, he seemed intent on hitting someone else. He drew back a fist.

Instantly, Cole had the tip of his Bowie knife at the Frenchman's throat. The sister gasped. The Frenchman froze, his fist cocked back by his ear.

Finally, the lieutenant took action. He put a restraining hand on Cole's arm. "Hey, everybody calm down. Cole, put down that knife." To the Frenchman he said, "*Calmez-vous.*"

Cole sheathed the knife, figuring that stabbing the brother would not win him the sister's favor. The Frenchman dropped his hands to his sides, although his eyes clearly showed that he would like nothing better than to pummel Cole.

Cole had to give the brother credit. He looked more angry than afraid. Maybe he really was a Resistance fighter.

Vaccaro seemed relieved that Cole had put the knife away, but he wanted his own slice of the Frenchman. "Tough guy, huh? Where were you four years ago when the Germans marched right in?"

His insults fell on deaf ears. Without a proper translator, they had to do their best to communicate using the lieutenant's college French. The young woman, whose name was Lisette, made it clear that she did not know the whereabouts of the German sniper. She also made it abundantly clear that she had no interest in seeing him again.

"*Bâtard*," she hissed at the mention of Rohde's name.

It evolved that what Lisette was most concerned about was getting back to the farm and to her niece, Elsa, who was in the care of an elderly neighbor. Already, the day was getting late. No way was Lisette going to make it there before sunset, and the last thing she needed to do was to go wandering around the countryside after dark, not with Germans, Polish troops, and trigger-happy Americans shooting at anything that moved. Reluctantly, Lisette agreed to spend the night at the American command post for Leo's sake, if not her own. In the morning, the lieutenant told her that Cole would escort her home.

"He will get you there safely, if anyone can," Mulholland said.

Henri managed to explain that he needed more ammunition for his rifle. Cole was surprised to see that the Frenchman carried a battered but well-cared for Springfield. It must have been a relic from the Great War, but would be a thorn in the side of the Germans, all the same.

In English and broken French, Lieutenant Mulholland explained to Henri that the Americans were low on ammunition due to the supply lines being stretched thin. Cole gave him a couple of clips from his utility belt. Who knew, maybe the Frenchman would do some good with the rounds of

.30/06. The more Germans that he shot, the fewer that the Americans would have to worry about.

Cole was getting low on ammo himself, and hoped that they would be resupplied soon. Then again, it suited Cole just fine if there weren't any bullets to waste. That was how he had been raised to think, back home in the mountains.

Henri gave his sister one last disapproving look, shouldered his rifle, and headed out to rejoin the Resistance fighters.

By some miracle, the farm that was serving as the forward command post still had a working telephone, and Lieutenant Mulholland got Lisette a few minutes on the phone to call home with the news that she would return in the morning.

Any ideas that Cole and Vaccaro had about keeping the French girl company were quickly squelched by the lieutenant.

"I'll see to it that the mademoiselle is comfortable for the night in our HQ here," Mulholland said. "Cole, you and Vaccaro and Harper had better take the first shift of sentry duty. There's no telling who's out there."

"Yes, sir," Vaccaro said, answering for all three of them. As soon as Mulholland was out of earshot, he grinned and mimicked the lieutenant's self-important tone. " 'I'll see to it that the mademoiselle is comfortable.' You bet your ass he will!"

* * *

FRUSTRATED, Rohde pressed his luck and crept within range of the American command post. Through his binoculars, he could see Lisette, and Leo—and the hillbilly sniper, all talking together.

He was too far for an effective shot, and thought about moving closer. To his disappointment, however, he saw the

American sniper move back out into the woods and fields, most likely to do some hunting of his own.

Rohde could have wreaked havoc on the command post, picking off an officer or two, but he felt too exposed. Besides, without any confirmation, they would not be counted toward his official record. Why take the risk? The area was swarming with Allied troops, not to mention the fact that the American sniper was out there somewhere, surely eager to get Rohde in his sights.

Planes kept appearing overhead, making it difficult to move undetected across the roads and fields. The American planes were not above strafing a lone German soldier, especially if they had any inkling that he was a sniper.

In the relative safety of the falling dusk, Rohde worked his way back toward Lisette's farm. He did not know why, nor did he have any particular reason, other than that it was on the route toward the German base. He could see that the farm was going to be in the path of the battle to come.

Rohde approached the farmhouse stealthily. No one seemed to be around.

The old dog came out to greet him, not even bothering to bark because he knew Rohde by now; he had been laying in the cool dirt. Rohde scratched his ears.

He approached the house and peeked in a window, rifle at the ready. No sign of Lisette's brother, the Resistance fighter, at least. No sign of Lisette, either. He did see an old woman at the table, and the little girl, Elsa.

Rohde opened the door without bothering to knock. The old woman looked up, clearly startled. Elsa shouted his name happily, apparently unaware of the fact that he was responsible for her brother's disappearance. The old woman looked at her in surprise.

"Lisette?" he asked. There was no point in trying to

communicate at any length with the old woman, but she could surely understand that much.

"*Demain matin*," the old lady blurted, with a glance at the telephone in the kitchen. "*Elle a dit que un sniper va marcher ici.*"

"*Un sniper? Ici?*"

"*Oui. Demain matin.*" The old woman nodded emphatically, almost fiercely. He realized that she had emphasized the sniper's arrival to scare him off.

Tomorrow morning. That was all Rohde needed to know. He turned and left.

He had glimpsed Lisette and the hillbilly sniper together at a distance at the American command post. What other sniper could the old woman possibly mean? On the walk back to headquarters, he wondered at his good fortune.

Come tomorrow morning, he was going to end this duel, once and for all.

CHAPTER THIRTY

WHEN ROHDE RETURNED to the base that evening, he learned that Hauptmann Fischer had sent for him. Having missed his chance at the American sniper, Rohde already felt frustrated by the day's events. He hoped for better luck tomorrow in ambushing the American at Lisette's farmhouse. Meanwhile, he was not eager to make his report to the Hauptmann.

With some trepidation, he waited outside Fischer's makeshift office, listening to him shouting at a sergeant over some infraction. Fischer's tendency to shout had become more frequent; it was easy to see that the stress of the war was getting to him.

Fortunately, Fischer seemed to have calmed down by the time Rohde was standing at attention before him. The Hauptmann was pleased when Rohde explained that he had set out early that morning and ambushed a squad of Americans nearby. Of course, Rohde left out the bit about using the French boy as bait, or about his encounter with the American sniper. With the Hauptmann being so touchy, the less said, the better.

But Fischer had not summoned him for small talk. The Hauptmann was clearly distracted and only half listening to Rohde's report. After a few moments, the Hauptmann came around to what was on his mind.

"It was a strange thing, what happened with old Hohenfeldt," Fischer said.

Rohde stiffened. He thought it best to pretend that he knew nothing about it. "What do you mean?"

"He was found in the latrine area early this morning. Apparently, he shot himself."

"Suicide?" Rohde asked carefully, trying to put a note of surprise in his voice.

"Who would have thought it? Our old *Staber* was as solid as they come. All he cared about were guns and bullets."

"And requisition forms," Rohde muttered, then added more loudly, "War changes people."

"It does, doesn't it?" The Hauptmann looked more intently at Rohde. "War changes a boy from Mannheim into a killer, for example."

"If you say so, sir." Rohde was a little taken aback that the Hauptmann knew where he had grown up, but of course, that had been one of the questions answered by Major Dorfmann's propaganda article.

"The curious thing about Hohenfeldt was that he apparently shot himself, but was found with the pistol in his right hand. He was left-handed, you see."

"That is strange, sir." Rohde felt a trickle of sweat begin under his armpits, suddenly aware of how stifling Fischer's office was in the summer heat. "Maybe the Resistance had something to do with it."

"You think so? How curious that the French would sneak into the latrine and target Hohenfeldt, of all people." Fischer looked intently at him. "I was told that you were seen with him last night at the armory, and that you were seen again at the armory this morning when Hohenfeldt was not there."

"Yes, sir."

Fischer frowned when Rohde did not elaborate. "Well, what were you doing there?"

Rohde did not like the way that Fischer seemed ready to pounce upon his answer, like a cat on a mouse. Who had seen him with Hohenfeldt and then told the story to the Hauptmann? It had to be one of the young *Soldaten* that he had seen working there. "He was issuing me the new Gewehr 43. This morning, I realized that I needed more ammunition, but the *Staber* was not there."

"Really? He finally gave you that rifle? He was guarding that thing like it was his mistress." Rohde could not help but wince at the choice of words. Fischer went on, "What did Hohenfeldt say to you when he gave you the rifle last night? Did he give any indication that he was suicidal?"

"No, sir. He simply said that he wanted to see me put it to good use." Rohde kept his voice carefully neutral. He did not like the direction this conversation was taking. It was beginning to feel too much like an interrogation.

"I see," Fischer said doubtfully. "I have to say, Rohde, how curious it is that you ended up with that rifle, and Hohenfeldt ended up dead."

Rohde felt as if he was getting boxed into a corner. An idea came to him. "He did say one thing, sir. Something about how, now that I had a new rifle, that perhaps you would like to have the other sniper rifle for your personal use."

"He said that?"

"Yes, sir."

The Hauptmann studied him thoughtfully, taking a moment to think that over. "You are a slippery one, aren't you, Rohde? It's as if there is always a chess game going on in that head of yours. If you give up a pawn, can you capture a rook? Perhaps that is what makes you a good sniper."

No, Rohde did not like where this was going at all. He thought desperately for a way to get Fischer off his back. "Come with me tomorrow, sir. I am setting up an ambush for the American sniper."

"You mean the one that Dorfmann claimed you already shot?" Fischer gave a wry smile.

"That was Major Dorfmann's article, sir. Not mine."

"That is true, Rohde. Unfortunately, you and I both know that words don't kill. Only bullets do that. Do you know where this American sniper will be?"

Rohde leaped right into it, knowing that any hesitation would come off as false to the Hauptmann, with whom he had already pushed his luck. "There was a boy who got lost, and the Americans found him. They're bringing the boy back home in the morning."

"How would you know about that?"

"I know the boy's aunt." Rohde let slip a knowing smile.

"You would, wouldn't you?" Fischer knew that Rohde wouldn't have been the first soldier in his unit to consort with a French girl.

"Help me ambush him, sir. Together, we can get him."

Rohde saw from the way that the Hauptmann hesitated, that Fischer thought he should refuse. He was an officer, not a sniper. And he did not seem quite convinced about the business with Hohenfeldt. But Fischer always had expressed some fascination with sniping. The temptation was too much.

"In the morning?"

"Yes, sir. With your permission, I will stop by the armory and get my old rifle. Of course, it is your choice which rifle you should use."

"The Mauser is fine. You use the new one. You are a much better shot than I am, anyway."

Rohde smiled and laid it on as thick as he dared. "I don't know about that, sir. I have seen you shoot. In the morning, you and I will teach the Americans a lesson. Maybe they will put us both in for an Iron Cross."

Fischer's mood had been improving at the thought of doing something as simple as going into the field. He scowled at the mention of the medal. "Don't you ever give up, Rohde? You and your damn medal!"

Rohde drew himself up straighter. He struggled, without much success, to keep his voice calm. That medal meant everything to him. "I have already earned that medal ten times over, sir. There are snipers who have not killed nearly as many enemies as I have who have the Iron Cross."

Ordinarily, a mere enlisted man such as Rohde would never dare to address an officer in that tone or to express such thoughts. But he and Fischer had a history together. The Hauptmann's patience, however, had its limits.

"Do not lecture me, Rohde! It is up to your commanding officer when and if you should be nominated for the Iron Cross. Many men have done much here. There are more than snipers under my command."

"Major Dorfmann said that he would nominate me."

Rohde's petulant tone caused Fischer's face to turn red, and a vein pulsed just above the tight collar of the Hauptmann's tunic. He drew in a breath as if to shout, then gulped it back, and instead said in a low voice that was far more menacing, "Let me tell you something, Rohde. Dorfmann wanted to put you in for the Iron Cross. He would do it in a heartbeat, for the sake of publicity. But I told him not to. How do you like that? If I were not here, you could go to Dorfmann and he could get you your piece of tin. Until then, you must still prove yourself to me. I still believe in a thing called a soldier's honor. Do you have honor, Rohde?"

Rohde took a deep breath and struggled to control the

rage that must be showing on his face. How could Fischer deny him that medal?! "Of course I have honor, sir."

"Do you? I wonder." Fischer sighed. "Meet me here tomorrow morning with that sniper rifle, and we will do our duty without concerning ourselves about glory and medals. You are dismissed, Rohde."

* * *

TEN MINUTES LATER, Rohde was back at the armory to retrieve his old Mauser K98 for the Hauptmann's use. His conversation with Hauptmann Fischer had left him both angry and nervous. The thought that Fischer was denying him the Iron Cross left him stunned. If it had not been for the Hauptmann, his medal might already be on its way from Berlin.

As if that wasn't bad enough, Fischer seemed to suspect that he'd had something to do with old Hohenfeldt's death. If there had been anything more than mere suspicions, Rohde was sure that he would already be under arrest. Still, Fischer's doubts weren't going to help Rohde get his medal any sooner.

His one chance at redemption seemed to be bagging that American sniper tomorrow. Rohde hated to put all of his eggs in that basket. Anything might happen.

No one seemed to have been put in charge of the armory yet, but a young *Soldat* was on duty, loading bullets into clips. Rohde recognized him from that morning.

He looked up as Rohde came in, a frisson of fear showing in his eyes. Rohde glared at him, and the soldier looked away.

Rohde found his old rifle just where he had left it in the Staber's office. The darkened armory smelled reassuringly of gun oil and cool metal. No wonder old Hohenfeldt had liked being armorer so much.

With one item of business taken care of, Rohde moved on

to take care of the next. He walked over to where the *Soldat* was working and picked up one of the clips as if to inspect it, and then loaded the K98 he had just retrieved. He put the muzzle against the boy's forehead. The soldier's eyes grew big as *Hundermarken* discs. One twitch of Rohde's finger and his brains would be scattered across the armory.

"Next time, mind your own business and keep your mouth shut, if you know what's good for you," Rohde said. "Understand?"

The frightened Soldat managed to nod, even with Rohde grinding the muzzle into his skull. When he lowered the rifle, there remained an indentation in the young soldier's forehead.

"Good," Rohde said. "Now, tell me where old Hohenfeldt kept his supply of explosive bullets."

Strictly speaking, explosive bullets were not used by snipers working to halt the Allied advance. But on the Eastern Front, where the fighting between Germans and Russians took on a hateful aspect, the explosive B-Patrone 7.92×57mm Mauser ammunition was used by snipers. Technically, explosive rounds were banned by the Geneva Convention, which specified the use of jacketed, non-explosive bullets. In any case, regular bullets were effective enough. Just ask any of the hundreds of thousands slain by them. When it came to the war in the East, however, there were no rules. German and Russian snipers alike used explosive ammunition when they could get their hands on it.

The hollow bullets were filled with an explosive mixture and designed to detonate on impact. For maximum effect, snipers on the Eastern Front often aimed at bony areas to ensure that detonation. Like a compact bomb, the explosion within the body was enough to shatter bone or hollow out a chest cavity. There was no walking away from a hit by an explosive round. But more than anything else, the exploding bullets created fear in the enemy.

Such ammo made snipers even more terrifying and deadly.

The explosive bullets were hard to come by. But even here in France, Rohde didn't doubt that the *Staber* had gotten his hands on at least a few rounds.

Sure enough, the *Soldat* went to a shelf and took down a box.

Rohde shoved the box into his haversack and nodded at the Soldat, who seemed to relax. That's when Rohde smashed the butt of the rifle into the young soldier's belly.

He grabbed a few handfuls of regular 7.92 mm rounds, and then stalked out of the armory, leaving the *Soldat* gasping on the floor, doubled up in pain.

Rohde had ammo, and he had a rifle for Hauptmann Fischer. Before dawn, the two of them would set an ambush for the American sniper at Lisette's farmhouse.

CHAPTER THIRTY-ONE

LIEUTENANT MULHOLLAND MUST NOT HAVE GOTTEN ANYWHERE with the mademoiselle, because just after first light, it was Cole and Harper who escorted her back to her farmhouse near Argentan. Vaccaro was to stay behind with the rest of the squad.

"Why does Cole get all the gravy jobs?" Vaccaro groused.

"You heard what the captain said, Vaccaro. All hell is about to break loose around here," Mulholland said. "Cole might actually have a chance of getting that girl home, and getting back here again. Until he does, we need someone to scout the territory and shoot back at any snipers."

Leaving the command post behind, Cole and Harper made their way through a countryside that echoed with the chatter of machine-gun fire and the *pop, pop, pop* of rifles. Every now and then, the country air was shattered by the *whump* of field artillery or tank fire. The whole battle seemed to be heating up, and here they were, walking right into it.

"I don't like this one bit," Harper said. He was jumpy and nervous, his finger not far from the trigger of his rifle. He was armed with a Springfield rifle with iron sights, in respect of the fact that he was by de facto a scout, rather than a sniper. Cole nodded, his eyes busy scanning the landscape, his sniper's senses on high alert. "I sure do feel like we dragged this girl and the kid out of the frying pan, and now we are tossing them into the fire. This whole damn countryside is about to go to hell. But she's got to get back to her niece."

"Once she's got the kids, she ought to get out of Dodge," Harper agreed.

"Yeah, but where would she go? In any direction, she could run into German troops or smack dab into a firefight. She can't stay with the squad because God only knows what we're in for. Maybe what she ought to do is hunker down and wait it out down in the root cellar. I wish I knew enough French to tell her that."

There really wasn't an ideal solution. From the sounds they kept hearing around them, the entire countryside seemed to be engulfed in fierce running battles. Back at the temporary HQ, the lieutenant had made it clear that Allied forces were converging on the Falaise area, where the Wehrmacht was making a last stand. It seemed as if Lisette's farmhouse would be close to the action.

"You two need to escort her back to the safety of her farmhouse, and then get the hell out of there," Mulholland had said. "If you don't, there's a good chance you might find yourselves on the wrong side of enemy lines. Everything is really fluid right now."

Listening to the sounds of fighting, and seeing the smoke filling the skies, Cole had to agree.

He insisted on going first, although Lisette still managed to guide them down the narrow dirt roads, keeping a firm grip on her nephew's hand. They rounded a bend in the road, and there was the farmhouse. White-washed and neatly thatched, Cole thought it looked like something out of a postcard.

Lisette let go of the boy's hand, and he raced toward the house. An old woman came to the front door that faced the road, with a little girl tangled in the woman's voluminous skirts.

Lisette gestured for them to come inside. The two soldiers did so, removing their helmets out of politeness as they went in. The kitchen they found themselves in was small and cramped. Cole was surprised, on closer inspection, that the floor was of hard-packed dirt; even his family's rough cabin in Gashey's Creek had a floor of rough-sawn boards.

The old lady looked at the two GIs with alarm, clutching her old sweater tighter against her ample body. Cole realized it was probably the first time she had seen an American up close. For the last few years, the only soldiers in these parts had worn German uniforms.

If Mulholland's French back at HQ had been rudimentary, the language skills of the two GIs was nonexistent. Lisette smiled and gestured as if she wanted to give them coffee, but mostly she seemed relieved to be back with both children. The old lady began gathering up her things as if to go, but Lisette seemed to be encouraging her to stay. He caught the French word, *dangereux*.

Cole felt that they had done their duty. It was time to get back to the war.

They managed to decline the coffee with smiles and by saying, "No, no."

Cole wondered if they could go out the kitchen door, out into the farmyard. He pointed at it, and Lisette nodded.

They stepped out into the farmyard and had walked a few yards from the house. Cole thought he heard something, or *felt* something, like he was being watched. The hair on the back of his neck stood on end, and he turned to look over his shoulder.

From across the farmyard, someone shot at them.

Harper went down.

* * *

"GOT HIM, GOT HIM, GOT HIM!" Fischer shouted in excitement.

Rohde was impressed, in spite of himself. He and the Hauptmann had set up before dawn and lain there for hours in hopes of a shot at the Americans.

When he had seen the hillbilly sniper with the flag on his helmet escorting Lisette and the boy, he could not believe his good luck at how things had worked out. Finally, here was the chance to cement Rohde's reputation as a sniper.

Fischer had insisted on waiting until the Americans came back out of the farmhouse—alone. He did not want the woman or the boy to be in the line of fire. Rohde had no such compunctions, but he did not argue.

They had agreed that Rohde would shoot the American hillbilly sniper. Fischer would shoot the other one.

At the last instant before Rohde's own rifle had fired, the American had shifted position, turning to look in Rohde's direction—almost as if he had eyes in the back of his head.

Rohde missed.

He fired again, but the hillbilly was already behind cover.

Fischer had more luck. The other American was dead.

And now they had the hillbilly sniper pinned down.

Rohde had an entire clip loaded with the explosive bullets he had stolen from the armory. He had been reluctant to use the forbidden ammunition with Fischer present, but there was no way that he was going to miss out on the opportunity to use it now. Quickly, he swapped out the clip of standard ammunition in the Gewehr 43 for the explosive rounds.

One hit, even on an extremity, would shatter a limb with deadly effect.

* * *

COLE DOVE for cover and kept his head down as bullets struck the water trough. Once the firing stopped, he risked a peek at Harper's body, lying still in the tall grass nearby.

He had liked Harper. He had known him for a short time, but a flood of emotions washed over him: fear, anger, sadness at another life wasted. He forced himself to stay focused. The important thing now was to stay alive himself.

Cole couldn't have asked for better cover than the stone water trough. He got down low near the base, glad that the thing looked heavy enough to stop a Panzerfaust round. Back home, the cows had to settle for drinking out of a rusty bathtub or tin trough. French farmers did it right. He took a gander around the side of the stone trough and saw not one, but two, German snipers. One was using the top of the wall on the opposite side of the farmyard to rest his rifle upon. The other sniper was much better hidden. Cole could barely see the other man's rifle, jutting from the bottom edge of the wall.

One of them had to be Rohde. This was clearly an ambush. What sniper other than Rohde would have any reason to visit this farm? It was too much of a coincidence, and Cole didn't believe in coincidences. You couldn't, not if you wanted to stay alive out here.

Rohde. This was the sniper who had staked the boy in the field. This was the sniper who had almost killed him, firing from that barn outside St. Dennis de Mere. Some of Cole's calm demeanor began to slip. His heart rate sped up from a mixture of anticipation and fear. One of them would not be leaving this place alive.

Cole pushed any doubts aside. He replaced those emotions with a calm resolve, or maybe call it a dead certainty. He was going to kill whoever had shot Harper.

ON THE OTHER side of the farmyard, the Germans couldn't wait to get a shot at Cole.

"Sir, can you see him?" Rohde whispered. "It is the American sniper. You saw his helmet. Just think what it will mean if we can bag him. Do you see him?

"No. Maybe. I am not sure."

"I think he is wounded. I almost have him in my sights. Can you tell me if he is moving at all?"

Fischer had proven that he was not a bad shot, but he was far from being an experienced sniper. In his excitement, the Hauptmann raised his head to get a better look. Looking on, Rohde started to warn the Hauptmann to keep his head down, but then bit back the words. Rohde was not about to forget that it was Fischer who had withheld his Iron Cross.

* * *

AS COLE WATCHED, one of the Germans raised his head above the wall they were hiding behind, as if to get a better view of Harper's body. It was the kind of dumb move a greenhorn made.

Cole thought at first that it must be a trick, maybe a helmet on a stick, trying to get him to reveal himself. They must have thought Cole was a dumb Jasper, if ever there was one.

He looked more closely, surprised to see that it was an actual head, on an actual German. The distance across the farmyard was not very great, and through the scope, Cole could see the man's face. Cole put his crosshairs on the German's *medulla oblongata* and pulled the trigger.

The bullet smashed through the bridge of the German's nose. His body slumped across the wall.

Instantly, two shots in rapid succession struck the water trough, one bullet striking just an inch from Cole's face, sending stone chips into his eye. The bullet had not just struck, he realized, it had *detonated*. There had been a small but unmistakable explosion, like a powerful firecracker going off. What the hell was the German shooting at him with?

He rolled away from the base of the trough, blinking furiously, temporarily blinded.

He had two thoughts. First, he hoped to hell that he would be able to see again. A blind sniper wasn't worth a damn. Next, he knew for damn sure that it wasn't Rohde that he'd shot. Hadn't looked like him, for one thing. Hadn't acted like him, for another. Killing Rohde would have been too damn lucky, anyhow.

No, Rohde had used the other sniper as bait. Cole was a little shocked at that. Could Rohde really be that ruthless, letting one of his own get shot just for a chance at Cole? The thought was chilling. Then again, this was the same sniper who had staked a boy out in the middle of a battlefield, giving it no more thought than if he'd put out a jar of honey to trap flies.

Now, the German seemed to be using explosive bullets. Cole had heard rumors about such bullets, but thought that they were banned.

As Cole turned it over in his mind, he didn't feel fear. He felt the slow burn of anger. He'd nail that son of a bitch's hide to the barn door yet.

"Cole!"

Lisette? At the sound of the French girl calling his name, any sense of calm evaporated. His heart hammered in his chest. She shouted his name again.

She must have heard the sound of shooting in her farmyard and come out to investigate. Cole couldn't decide if that was brave, or dumb. Right now, he was leaning toward dumb.

With a sinking feeling, he realized that the whole damn situation had gone si-goggly. The water trough was positioned in such a way that he could see Lisette, but that she could not see *him*. The French girl could not see Harper's dead body or the German's either, for that matter.

She was walking right into Rohde's line of fire.

There was no way for Cole to signal Lisette without getting picked off, and his command of French did not go much beyond *non* or *oui*. Once she came around the corner of the cottage, Rohde was going to shoot her for the hell of it, and there wasn't a goddamn thing that Cole could do about it.

Unless. He peered around the base of the water trough through blurry eyes. His left eye stung like hell; there was a piece of stone in there that felt as big around and sharp as an arrowhead, but Cole did his best to ignore it. Wasn't his shooting eye, at least. The rest of his body tensed up as he got ready to make a move.

"You're a dang fool, Micajah Cole," he muttered to himself.

Then Cole leaped up and ran.

He dodged left and right, jackrabbiting across the field, away from the farmhouse. A bullet plucked at his sleeve, but he kept going. If being a sniper had taught him anything, it was how to make himself hard to hit. There was a time to walk proud, and a time to run like a rabbit.

Another shot, and another. That goddamn Kraut had hisself a semiautomatic rifle.

It was one thing to dodge a sniper with a bolt action rifle, and quite another to get shot at by a sniper with a weapon that dispensed a bullet with each pull of the trigger. An explosive bullet, at that.

Got to keep moving. He headed for the laundry hanging on the line, saw a bullet shred a sheet, and kept sprinting. Some low bushes grew at the edge of the yard and he crouched down as he ran. The next three bullets ripped the air overhead.

Then Cole was in among the woods beyond the barn. A bullet exploded against a tree, scattering bark and splinters. The shooting stopped. He wondered if Rohde had followed him, but didn't slow down long enough to look over his shoulder. More shots answered his question. Rohde was coming after him.

So far, the bullets had gone wild, which meant that Rohde didn't have a clear shot. Cole juked left and right, bobbing and weaving as he ran, doing his best impression of a cottontail rabbit. He knew from experience that hitting a running target meant that the shooter had to anticipate the space that the target was going to occupy next. He didn't plan on giving Rohde that opportunity. Still, that hardly meant Cole didn't feel a tingling between his shoulder blades, as if he had a paper target pinned there.

Another bullet hit a tree and exploded, too close for comfort. At the edge of the woods, he hit a tangle of briers that clawed at his clothes and bare skin. He managed to push on through, but not without shredding his uniform in a couple of places.

He emerged into a field. Not much cover here, but if he could just get into some tall grass, he could take a prone position and ambush Rohde as he—

Cole never finished the thought. Immediately to his left, he became aware of a metallic rumbling and clanking. Fleeing from Rohde had given him tunnel vision.

He hadn't even noticed that there was a German Tiger tank coming right at him.

CHAPTER THIRTY-TWO

WEIGHING FIFTY TONS, a Tiger tank was a formidable beast with armor several inches thick, treads three feet across, and a cannon the size of a tree trunk. The sight of it turned Cole's heart into a trip hammer inside his chest. The thing was churning toward him.

All thoughts of Rohde vanished. Cole had more immediate concerns. Like staying alive for the next sixty seconds.

Against that behemoth, his rifle would be of no more use than a peashooter. The only thing that Cole could think to do was to get out of the way. He dodged right and ran, but it didn't do him much good. Moving in tandem on the Tiger's flank was a second German tank.

Though slower than a Sherman tank, the massive panzers still moved faster than Cole could sprint at top speed. For a fleeting moment, he feared that he would be run over and crushed. He felt like some animal caught trying to cross a backcountry road, hoping to avoid becoming roadkill while some bootlegger's car bore down on him relentlessly.

He had seen more than a few guys run over by tanks.

What was left of them resembled persimmon jelly. Oozing in the bottom of a tank track.

Hell of a way to go.

Just then, both tanks clanked to a halt.

It soon became clear why the panzers had stopped. It certainly wasn't to avoid running Cole down. There must be men inside the tanks, but the machines seemed as monstrous to him as a boot must look to an ant.

Above the rumble of the tank engines, he heard the whine of their big guns being positioned. He could see that the guns were elevated too high to be aimed at him. Besides, no panzer crew was going to waste a shell on a lone soldier, sniper or not.

Cole ran harder, thinking that he was going to make it across the field.

That's when the first panzer, the one closest to him, opened fire.

Considering that the 88 mm cannon was no more than fifty feet away, the sensation was like the world was exploding. Flame stabbed from the muzzle. The blast was deafening, so loud that it was like a physical wave washing over him. He actually stumbled.

That's when the second tank fired.

Cole kept running, sensing rather than hearing someone hollering. He realized that the hollering was coming from him. This wasn't a sound of fear, but more like a primal scream of defiance.

When he spotted an old shell hole ahead, he dove down into it.

To his left, he was dimly aware of another ear-splitting cannon blast. He looked in that direction and saw not one, but *two* Sherman tanks emerge from a copse of brushy, second-growth trees.

The large white stars on the tanks, designating them as

U.S. Forces, might even have been a welcome sight if he hadn't been caught practically in the middle of a tank battle.

Cole wished that he could help, but the best that he could do right now was to keep his head down. He reached for his utility belt, thinking to reload—but it wasn't there. He must have lost it somewhere between Lisette's farm and the shell hole. Maybe in that tangle of briers? It was a hell of a thing, but there was no going back to look for it now, which meant that he was down to the bullets in his clip. He had, what, two bullets left?

As he watched, the other Sherman fired, the shell hitting the thickly plated front of the Tiger and *karooming* off. That was one hell of a ricochet. The sound itself was terrifying, but not nearly as frightening as the thought that the shell from the direct hit had bounced harmlessly off the panzer.

Then the panzer fired again.

This time, the Germans' aim was better. The round hit almost dead center in the turret, peeling back the three-inch armor as easily as a can opener.

Bullseye, Cole thought, mesmerized by the sight.

The game little Sherman bounced on its treads as fire erupted through every seam and joint in the armor plating, like a tin can with a firecracker going off inside. While the German rounds tended to be solid, they had a nasty habit of igniting the fuel supply in the gasoline-powered Sherman tanks. The hatch popped open. Cole understood that tanks held a crew of four, but just one man came out. The German shell must have killed the other three.

The lone escapee from the burning tank was on fire.

Burning gasoline from the detonation had coated his clothes so that he flamed like a six-foot torch. The screaming was awful. He had seen men burn to death before, and knew that death came too slowly.

Cole couldn't bear it. He shot the man, ending the tanker's suffering instantly.

The soldier fell to the ground and lay still, flames licking over him. The sickeningly sweet smell of cooked flesh reached Cole's nostrils.

One bullet left.

Now the tanks opened fire upon each other again, making the air feel as if it was being ripped apart. The noise made it difficult to breathe. He had to get the hell out of there. He was still in the shell hole, so he climbed out and got to his feet.

The three remaining tanks maneuvered for position, the faster and nimbler Sherman trying to get around behind the panzers, where the thinner armor plating gave the Americans some chance of destroying the German tank. Off to the side, Cole felt like a spectator at a football game—only this game had deadly consequences.

That's when he happened to look across the field and saw a figure looking back at him. Rohde. Had to be. He wore the same camouflage pattern uniform. Cole had damn near forgotten about him in the confusion of the tank battle. But Rohde had not forgotten about *him*.

As Cole watched, Rohde raised his rifle and aimed in his direction. A bullet snapped past, then another. Wasted shots. Some part of Cole scoffed. Where he came from, you didn't waste a bullet.

Maybe Rohde wasn't as good a shot as everyone made him out to be. Then again, with the semi-automatic sniper rifle, maybe he didn't have to be. Another bullet tore the air, close to Cole's head. Cole's spine tingled involuntarily. Rohde was walking in his bullets.

Cole did not have that luxury. He had one bullet. One chance. The distance was about 300 feet. Farther than he would have liked for an offhand shot.

He took a breath, held it, and set the crosshairs on the enemy sniper. Another shot zipped past, this one so close that it seemed to pluck at his buttons. He ignored that and blocked out everything, even the grinding tanks, now just yards away.

Cole fired.

Through the scope, he watched Rohde go down.

The hit felt right, but there was no time to make certain that Rohde was dead. No sooner had Cole taken his eye from the scope, then he saw one of the panzers angling right at him with multiple tons of steel and whirring treads. Like an afterthought, the panzer opened up with its machine gun, plowing the ground in front of him.

Cole did the smart thing, and ran.

His only thought was to get out of that killing field. Away from those tanks. Another hedgerow loomed ahead. He didn't know what was on the other side, but he was hopeful that it wouldn't be more German tanks.

Out of the corner of his eye, he detected more movement. He looked to his left. There must have been fifty German soldiers following in the wake of the panzers. Two of the soldiers spotted him and peeled away from the rest, running to get between Cole and the hedge, seemingly intent on capturing him.

Cole was glad that they hadn't decided to shoot him outright. But they were on a fool's errand if they thought that they were going to capture him. Cole had no intention of sitting out the rest of the war in some POW camp. Never mind the fact that he didn't like his chances if he got caught with a sniper rifle. Captured snipers on both sides had a funny habit of not making it to the rear.

Right now, that sniper rifle was out of ammo. He wished that he had stuffed a few clips in his pockets and not put it all in that goddamn utility belt. But like his pa used to say, shit in one hand and wish in the other, and see which one fills up first.

His only weapon was the Bowie knife. It didn't seem like much use against a German MP-40.

The soldiers ran faster, closing in on their quarry. The angle that they had been running at meant that they had less distance to cover to reach the hedge, and now they were between Cole and relative safety. The two were so close now that he could make out the details of their faces. They looked young but weather-beaten. Peachy stubble on their chins. Excitement lit their eyes. He noticed that one set of eyes was blue; the other was brown.

Both raised their weapons, expecting Cole to stop.

He charged toward them, his hand reaching for the antler handle of the Bowie knife. Cole let go of a rebel yell, high and keening, that froze both Germans in their tracks. The sound of it sent a shiver up his own spine.

He ran full tilt into the soldier on the right. The German was bigger than Cole, but Cole's momentum knocked the German off his feet. His helmet and his weapon went flying in different directions.

To his left, Cole heard the other German shouting something, waving the MP-40 at him. The German could have touched the trigger and killed him with a single burst, but still seemed intent on capturing him. Besides, if he fired now, he had an equal chance of killing the other German along with Cole. Cole crouched and pivoted, grabbing the muzzle and pointing it away with his left hand. In his right hand was the knife. The German's eyes got big at the sight of it. Cole had intended to stab him in the throat, but at the last instant he turned the knife and hit the German across the bridge of the nose with the brass guard. That German went down too.

Cole ran on, expecting at any moment to feel a bullet

punch between his shoulder blades. He ran fifty feet, and it felt like he was running a marathon.

Then he was in among the thick branches of the hedge, worming his way deeper through the tangle. The hedge was practically impenetrable, but Cole had no choice but to fight his way through. Dead branches clawed at his face and ripped his clothes. His rifle got tangled up, but he managed to yank it free with such force that the shoulder strap snapped.

He kept going until he burst through the far side of the hedge. He jumped the last few feet and landed in a heap.

He was in a new field. But he wasn't alone.

A whole squad of troops was looking at him in disbelief. One or two pointed weapons at him, but no one fired.

He saw at once they weren't Germans. They weren't Americans, either.

Still on his knees from his ignominious arrival in the field, Cole raised his hands, not sure what the hell he had gotten himself into.

Then a very large soldier stepped forward and offered Cole a paw the size of a catcher's mitt.

Not sure what else to do, Cole took it, and allowed himself to be hauled to his feet.

"American?" the man asked in passable English.

"As Yankee Doodle," Cole replied.

That seemed to please the big soldier, who grinned. "We are the 1st Polish Division," he explained. "We are part of the trap closing in on the Germans. The English are coming at them from the west, and your forces along with ours are coming at them from the east."

It was no surprise to Cole that a big fight was brewing, but he had thought that the real action was going to be a little farther to the west. Having survived the last few minutes, his thoughts turned to Lisette with her little niece and nephew, who were about to find themselves in the middle of a battlefield.

The Polish soldier interrupted Cole's thoughts. "What is on the other side of this hedge?" he asked. "You seemed in a hurry to get away."

"German panzers and at least a couple dozen troops that I could see. Maybe more."

"Well, we will wait for them to go by. We need the element of surprise to complete the encirclement. Meanwhile, I hope that I have answered your questions."

"I got just one more," Cole said. He nodded at the vehicles parked nearby. "Can I borrow one of them Jeeps?"

CHAPTER THIRTY-THREE

ROHDE TOUCHED HIS SIDE, then took his hand away, staring in disbelief at the blood running off his fingers. The sight of so much blood—his own blood—instantly made him feel lightheaded. Fear gripped him. Was he going to die?

He inspected the wound, noting the spreading stain across his tunic. If he could just get some help, perhaps he would be saved. He was still on his feet, after all.

"Just a scratch, Carl," he said, trying to reassure his brother, whose presence he suddenly felt. The bullet wound was much more than a scratch, but he did not want his brother to worry. "I will be fine."

Soldiers swarmed around him, rushing alongside the tanks moving to attack the American forces. He cursed the American sniper who had shot him. Deep down, Rohde had to admit that the man was good. But if he'd been better, Rohde would already be dead. If only the attack hadn't come between them, perhaps Rohde would have had another chance at the American sniper. Who was the better man? Now, it seemed like he would never know.

"Medic!" Rohde shouted, glancing around desperately for

one of their white helmets. Sometimes the medics also wore white tunics emblazoned with a red cross, making them look like medieval knights. None was in sight. "I need a medic!"

He tried to stop a soldier who was running past.

"You there, get me a medic!"

The soldier was young, hardly more than a boy, and looked terrified. His new uniform marked him as a recent replacement. "Are you hurt?" he asked stupidly. Then he saw Rohde's wound and his eyes grew big. The soldier's reaction told Rohde what he already knew.

A sergeant pushed between them. He gave the young soldier a shove. "Go! Go!" He turned to Rohde. "He can't help you, you damn idiot. Get to the rear, assuming we still have one. Or better yet, surrender to the Amis. You'd better throw away that sniper rifle first if you do that."

Then the sergeant ran on, rejoining the assault. Within a minute, Rohde was alone on the field.

Or not quite alone. Several other wounded men lay there, along with a burning Sherman tank. A charred body lay near the tank, still smoldering. Rohde detected the horrible smell of burned human flesh.

Quickly, Rohde made up his mind that he would not surrender. Prisoners of war did not receive the Iron Cross. He still held out some dim hope that the medal might be his. More than that, he'd be damned if he would give up the Gewehr 43 rifle that had cost him so much. His only choice was to do as the sergeant had suggested, which was to make his way to the rear.

What he needed was some sulfa powder, some clean bandages—and a drink of water. Then he'd be as good as new. At least, that is what he told himself.

Rohde slipped his arm through the sling of the rifle and started toward where he thought the rear must be located. He hadn't gone more than a hundred meters when he stopped. With each step, his insides threatened to leak out of the gunshot wound. He pressed a hand against it to keep everything in. His fingers could not stop the blood, however. No way was he going to reach the rear.

And there was no guarantee that he would find any help there. The final fight for Falaise had left the entire country-side in turmoil. The German field hospital could be a mile away. Or it might no longer exist.

However, Lisette's cottage was not that far away. She would have bandages and water. There, he could patch himself up enough to rejoin his own forces.

He turned around.

"No, Carl, she's not going to be happy to see me," he agreed. "I will get some bandages and be on my way. And something to drink. I am awfully thirsty."

Painfully, Rohde recrossed the field, careful to avoid the burned body and the flaming ruins of the tank. Even from a distance, on a summer day, he felt the heat radiating from the furiously burning hulk. This time, he definitely smelled the bodies in the flames. The smell caught in his throat and made him want to gag.

He entered the woods through which he had chased the American sniper not more than twenty minutes ago. His side definitely felt as if something was trying to squeeze out. He pressed harder, causing yet more blood to ooze between his fingers. He had to get some bandages on that wound, and fast.

Each step seemed harder and harder. The thought occurred to him that if he simply lay down here among the trees, his body might go undiscovered forever.

More blood leaked out of him, now almost black in color. Rohde realized that he was probably dying.

He paused and leaned against a tree. The woods felt peaceful.

"It wasn't like this for you, was it, Carl? They tied you to a post and made you wear a blindfold. Those SS bastards. I know that you were not a deserter. You were no coward."

When he looked up through the branches at the sky, everything seemed to circle and swirl above him. Black spots swam in his vision and fear came flooding back. He did not want to die. He pushed away from the tree and forced himself to keep going. As long as he kept moving, there was still some hope.

Then the farmhouse came into sight. There was the body of the American by the water trough. Farther off, Hauptmann Fischer still lay slumped across the low stone wall where they had lain in ambush. Otherwise, the farmhouse and surrounding barnyard appeared quiet and untouched.

As he approached the house, he was still fifty meters away when Lisette's old dog spotted him and barked a warning.

* * *

INSIDE THE COTTAGE, Lisette had been trying to calm everyone down. Just twenty minutes before, the two American soldiers had gone walking out the kitchen door, only to be shot at.

"Do you think that the soldiers are still out there?" Madame Pelletier asked, clutching the front of her sweater in one hand.

"No, I saw them run off."

Madame Pelletier did not look relieved. She sank into a kitchen chair, apparently with no thoughts of returning to her own home down the road. Who could blame her, now that the war had come to their little corner of the countryside?

"I should be going," Madame Pelletier said half-heartedly, as if reading Lisette's mind.

"Please stay here and help with the children," Lisette said, knowing full well that the old woman would accept. "In a little while, we shall have something to eat."

Lisette had no doubts that it had been Rohde who had ambushed the Americans. He had stopped by yesterday, looking for her, and unwittingly, old Madame Pelletier had informed the German that she had received a phone call informing her that Lisette would be back in the morning, escorted by two American snipers. Armed with that bit of intelligence, he must have laid his trap.

It was small consolation that a dead German lay across the stone wall on the other side of the barnyard. One of the Americans was now dead, lying in the dirt beside the water trough. The other soldier, named Cole—the one with the cold eyes—had escaped through the trees beyond the barn. From a distance, she had seen the German sniper pursue him. It had to have been Rohde.

She had not gotten a glimpse of his face, but there was something about the way that he moved that looked familiar. She and Rohde had been lovers, after all.

A shudder of revulsion ran through her at the thought.

The children did not appear overly concerned about events at the farm. They seemed to view it all as a big adventure. Even Leo seemed not too worse for wear, given all that he had been through. Children were more resilient in some ways than adults. It helped that the American GIs had spoiled him with attention, not to mention chocolate and chewing gum.

"*Tante*, we are hungry!" Sophie said. "Did you bring us something good to eat?

Lisette took a deep breath and tried to calm herself, ignoring that fact that there were two dead men in her yard. The Americans had, in fact, given her a few tinned goods to bring home, along with some more Hershey's chocolate. Sharp-eyed Sophie must have noticed.

"Yes, let's have something to eat. We may need our energy before the day is through."

She busied herself unpacking the cans, and handed Madame Pelletier a can opener. She noticed that the old woman's hands were shaking.

That's when she heard the dog begin to bark.

She had forgotten the dog was out there. He had run off at the sound of gunshots, but must have returned.

"What now?"

Leo was already at the door, and opened it before she could stop him.

Almost immediately, he slammed it shut. He turned to Lisette, his face ghostly white.

"The German sharpshooter is here!"

Rohde had returned. Did it mean that he had killed the American?

Lisette felt her blood run cold. She struggled to remain calm for the children's sake. Behind her, Madame Pelletier gasped.

What could Rohde want? Considering what he had done to her, and to the Americans who had helped her home, it could not be anything good.

A wave of emotions washed over Lisette, from shame to fear. Shame that she had allowed herself to become involved with the German sniper in exchange for food—and if she was honest with herself, to satisfy her own desires and expel her loneliness. Fear, because Rohde's return could only mean nothing good.

To her surprise, the emotion that she settled on was anger.

Rohde had come back to her house? To harm her niece and nephew? How dare he!

"Get under the table," she ordered the children. There was no time for them to hide anywhere else, but the thick tabletop would stop a bullet if the German came in shooting. "Now!"

Desperately, she looked around for something to defend herself. She realized that she still held a wooden spoon in her hand. She tossed it away.

In two steps, she was at the door into the hallway, which was normally open. Behind it, she kept the ancient shotgun that Henri used to scare off foxes. She grabbed the shotgun now. For safety's sake, the shells were kept on a high shelf, out of the reach of the children.

The shelf was higher than eye level, so Lisette reached up, but felt nothing but dust.

Her heart hammered in fear. Where were those shells?

Her hand searched farther back. Out in the yard, the dog barked more furiously.

She heard Rohde shout her name. He must be right outside the door.

There. She touched the scattered shells, knocking them to the kitchen floor in the process. Lisette practically dove after them.

She saw the children huddled under the table with Madame Pelletier. The old woman had taken refuge there as well. She had her eyes closed, and her lips moved silently. The old woman was praying.

Lisette picked up the shotgun. Her hands did not shake at all as she worked the lever to open the breech, just as Henri had taught her. She slid a shell into each barrel, and snapped the gun shut.

Then she opened the door.

There was Rohde. He staggered toward the house. He was bleeding heavily from an ugly wound in his belly. There was so much blood that his tunic looked black. The circle of dark blood was big as a dinner plate. He was a dead man walking. She felt no pity, but only anger at what he had done to her and to Leo.

Lisette screamed at him and leveled the shotgun.

* * *

ROHDE HAD NOT EXPECTED a warm welcome. He had thought that he would force himself inside and take the medical supplies that he needed. It had not occurred to him that perhaps he would not get inside at all, if that stout cottage door was locked against him. He knew that he lacked the strength to break it down.

Rohde was hurting now, getting weaker. He looked behind him and saw that he was leaving a trail of blood across the muddy farmyard. He was leaking that much.

He need not have worried about the door.

The thick door opened and Lisette stepped out. In her hands, she held the ancient shotgun she kept around to ward off foxes and hawks. Her face looked hard and set.

She held the shotgun at hip level, and pointed it right at him.

"Lisette?"

"*Batard!*" she screamed again.

With weakening hands, Rohde hurried to unsling his rifle.

* * *

AS IF IN A DAZE, Lisette watched Rohde raise his rifle, practically falling down from the effort. Was he actually going to shoot at her?

Rohde shouted something at her in German, but the words were unintelligible.

He was swaying wildly as if blown by some unseen wind,

but managed to get the rifle to his shoulder.

Lisette realized, with a sense of shock, that he was going to pull the trigger.

He fired.

The bullet struck the stone wall near her head and ricocheted away. Rohde really *was* trying to kill her.

The recoil of the rifle made him stagger. Reeling like a drunken man, covered in blood, Rohde was struggling to bring the rifle to bear once again.

Lisette did not give him a second chance. Bracing the shotgun against her hip, she leveled the gun at him and pulled both triggers at once.

* * *

TEN MINUTES LATER, a vehicle drove into the farmyard. Peering from the cottage window, Lisette recognized it as an American Jeep, similar to the ones that she had seen the day before at the command post. She did not, however, recognize the uniform of the soldier driving it, but she was relieved to see that he was not German.

Then the man in the passenger seat got out. She did recognize him—it was the American sniper, Cole. With a sense of relief, she could see that Rohde had not shot him, after all.

Cole was in a hurry, his rifle held at the ready. His eyes darted this way and that even as he crossed the barnyard. When he moved, he seemed to lope—almost like one of those foxes that emerged from the nearby woods.

He went over to the body of the GI at the water trough and removed ammunition from the dead man's utility belt. He straightened up, pressed a clip into his rifle, and moved toward the cottage door. He paused just long enough to give Rohde's body a glance.

Lisette opened the door just ahead of Cole. She was still holding the shotgun, loaded with fresh shells. Her ears still rang from the blast of the double barrels, but she was able to hear shooting and the deep boom of artillery. The firing was the closest that it had been.

Cole looked pointedly at the shotgun in her hands, and then out at what was left of Rohde.

"You OK?"

She knew what "OK" meant, and nodded.

"We need to get you and the young 'uns out of here," Cole said. "The whole dang war is headed this way."

Lisette did not really understand him.

Cole took a step back, waved at her with a *follow me* gesture, and then pointed at the Jeep. "*Maintenant*," he managed. "You and *les enfants*."

Although the words were mangled, Lisette understood the meaning well enough. She turned back into the kitchen and gathered Leo and Sophie. Old Madame Pelletier was still there, and there was no leaving her behind, so she was squeezed into the back seat of the Jeep next to the children. The dog would just have to fend for himself until they returned.

The driver shouted something in what sounded like Polish, and pointed toward the nearby field. He shouted again, an urgent tone in his voice.

At the last minute, Lisette remembered food and water and blankets for the children, and ran back into the kitchen. On the way, she had to pass Rohde's body again. Lisette had not wanted to look too closely, but she saw that the dual shotgun blasts had struck Rohde squarely in the chest. His tunic was a ruin, but his pretty, boyish face was untouched, other than having a final look of surprise upon it. His blue eyes stared.

She felt a stab of terrible regret, but had to remind herself that this dead young man had been *un monstre*, even if that was hard to equate with his appearance in death—a death that she had caused.

Lisette did not have time to search her emotions any further. She ran back to the kitchen, grabbing what she could. She had to abandon the shotgun to fill her arms. Cole ran after her, taking Lisette firmly by the arm and marching her back toward the Jeep.

Out of the corner of her eye, Lisette noticed movement in the field. Turning her attention there, she saw German troops, crouched low, crossing the field. As she watched, one of the soldiers pointed towards the farm and raised his rifle. He was going to shoot at them.

Lisette felt her insides go cold. All that she could think of was the children. *No, no. I will not lose Leo and Sophie.* She hurried to put herself between them and the German soldier.

Cole muttered something under his breath, put his rifle to his shoulder, and fired a shot. The German went down, buying them a little more time.

A few hours ago, Lisette might have gasped at the sight of a soldier being shot. Now she thought, *Good.*

More troops spilled from the woods and across the field. They heard the scream of a shell, and a geyser of earth erupted just beyond the barn.

Sophie and Madame Pelletier gave frightened cries, while Leo offered a boyish yelp of delight. It was all just so many fireworks to him.

Lisette scrambled into the back seat of the Jeep and took Sophie into her lap. Cole jumped in and slapped the driver on the shoulder. The Jeep spun momentarily in the mud, spitting dirt from its tires, then surged down the road, away from the oncoming assault.

CHAPTER THIRTY-FOUR

From the hills above the valley filled with German troops, artillery shells rained down. To the west was Canadian artillery, to the eastern side was Patton's 3rd Army. The Germans were effectively fish in a barrel.

The men in the artillery units stripped off their shirts and worked in the hot August sun, streaming sweat. Such destruction was hard work. Shells poured down into the valley below, killing and killing.

As the noose enclosed what was left of the German 7th army and 5th Panzer narrowed, artillery shells loaded with leaflets encouraging the Germans to surrender were fired into their positions. The sheets fluttered everywhere, snatched out of the air by desperate Wehrmacht troops. The SS threatened to shoot anyone they caught reading the leaflets.

Those who sensed the inevitable were likely hoping to stay alive long enough to do just what the leaflets suggested. Other Germans were focused on escaping. A few insisted on fighting—and dying—until the bitter end.

It was a point of consternation to many Allied officers that the bulging gap had not been pulled shut like the drawstring of a tobacco pouch, catching the Germans neatly inside. By now, just two miles of territory was left to German forces. Through this opening, the Wehrmacht continued to escape.

General Omar Bradley and the other Allied commanders had their reasons not to rush to close the gap, chief of which was worry over the confusion that might result among different units from different nations operating in close proximity in the heat of battle. Allied forces were arranged across from each other in what could easily become a circular firing squad. In their frenzy to kill Germans, they might very well kill one another. The Allied high command feared the toll that friendly fire would have on sensitive Allied alliances.

All in all, it was safer to let a few Germans escape than to take a chance that American, Canadian, Polish, and British troops might bombard one another by mistake.

In the middle of the artillery bombardment, an unusual drama unfolded.

Up on the heights, an American unit watched a German soldier galloping away on horseback. It was insanity that he would even try to cross that killing field. Machine-gun fire churned the narrow dirt road. At one point, a shell landed so close that dirt sprayed across horse and rider, but still they kept going.

Some of the soldiers stopped shooting and cheered him on.

With a last surge of power, horse and rider disappeared into the trees and relative safety.

A ragged cheer went up.

"What the hell's going on?" an officer wanted to know, red-faced. "How do you know that son of a bitch wasn't shooting at us on Omaha beach?"

"Sir, we just—"

"I don't want to hear it, soldier! Put some hurtin' on those sons of bitches!"

The firing recommenced.

It was likely that the horseman was trying to retreat down a road that would become known as "The Corridor of Death"—and with good reason. Dead horses, burned trucks, smashed tanks, and bodies—many, many bodies—lay thick on the road.

Thousands of fleeing troops using the one available road away from the Allies had to make their way across a narrow ford, known as the Gue de Moissy. In a sense, the Wehrmacht forces trying to cross the ford were like the camel trying to pass through the eye of a needle. Under relentless artillery fire and air attacks, somehow thousands of troops still managed to slip away. If there was a story to be told of courage under fire from this battle, it was at the ford. Their determination and order despite the chaos were some of the German Army's greatest accomplishments at Falaise, even in defeat.

The gap closed August 19 when U.S., British, Canadian, and Polish forces finally completed the Allied line. The tobacco pouch had been drawn shut.

The next day at 1200 hours the Normandy campaign was declared to be over. Seventy-seven days had passed since the D Day landing. Some thought that the war was essentially over after the disastrous German defeat, but that was wishful thinking. The fighting and dying would go on for another several months, with awful ordeals like the wintry Ardennes and Bastogne still ahead.

Around Falaise and Argentan, the numbers of dead were astonishing. At least 10,000 were killed. The Germans were comfortable with horses and had made use of them to pull wagons filled with supplies, or simply to ride. Now, dead horses lay everywhere. For days after the bombardment and retreat, witnesses described a gray haze over the valley. The haze came from swarms of flies settling over the dead men and horses. The unlucky men assigned to bury the dead sometimes had to shoot the bloated corpses to release enough of the putrid gas so that they could handle the bodies for burial. Some would suffer nightmares about such grisly sights for years to come.

With the battle won, General Eisenhower was one of those who came to tour the scenes of destruction. Much of Argentan, like other towns caught up in the fighting, lay in ruins. And yet, odd things had survived. Navigating the rubble, Ike's motorcade passed the bombed-out shell of a building, all of its windows shattered and the stucco pock-marked by bullets and shrapnel, but with its proud sign proclaiming "Ecole Maternelle" entirely intact.

Ike was awestruck by the human carnage. He later wrote, "The battlefield at Falaise was unquestionably one of the greatest killing fields of any of the war areas. Forty-eight hours after the closing of the gap I was conducted through it on foot, to encounter scenes that could be described only by Dante. It was literally possible to walk for hundreds of yards at a time, stepping on nothing but dead and decaying flesh."

With so many dead, it seemed miraculous that vast numbers of Germans somehow managed to survive the bombardment.

At least 20,000 and maybe more escaped into Germany.

Another 10,000 men became prisoners. Some might say they were the lucky ones, having survived the final battle and avoided the ones still to come. Long columns of prisoners marched endlessly with hands on heads, wearing greatcoats despite the summer heat. Veteran soldiers knew that come nightfall or winter, they would be glad of a coat.

Some Americans, out of curiosity, struck up conversations with the Germans, many of whom spoke some English. They found the Germans friendly, relieved that the war was over, and eager to talk about their families back home, as were the Americans. The soldiers had a great deal in common. Both sides came away from these conversations wondering what they'd been killing each other for.

EPILOGUE

MAJOR DORFMANN SAT at his desk, a glass of French cognac at his elbow. Sadly, France was lost. Happily, Dorfmann had managed to get out with several cases of very good cognac.

The cognac was for more than consumption; in a way, it was currency. He remembered the bad time after the Great War, when money itself had become worthless. A wheelbarrow full of paper money was needed to buy a loaf of bread. He suspected that those times were coming again. When that happened, the small bottles of cognac would be like gold for trading. Until then, he could afford to drink some of it and hope for better days. Besides, he needed a bit of alcoholic inspiration to generate his latest propaganda piece.

He sighed and sipped his cognac, enjoying the bite of it on his tongue, along with the faint taste of grapes and earth and sunshine mixed in with the heat of the alcohol. Better days, indeed.

Production of *Luftpost* by his SS Skorpion unit had been temporarily suspended in the confusion of the retreat from France, but he was proud of the fact that production had continued as soon as he returned to Germany and secured the use of a printing press. The Nazi war machine had run out of Luftwaffe airplanes, but it was not likely to run out of newsprint and printer's ink anytime soon. Airplanes would be welcome, but the weekly newspaper was almost as useful as powerful inspiration for the common soldier.

The newspaper that had permanently ceased production was *Lightning News: Condensed News for Service Men*. This was the paper he produced in English to be read by the Allies. Had his propaganda articles about girls back home in America being stolen by negroes and Jews made the GIs fight any less hard by undermining their confidence and doubting their government? Dorfmann liked to think so; there was real value in such fake news to undermine the democratic will. Without his *Lightning News*, France might have been lost sooner, or fewer Wehrmacht troops might have escaped the Falaise-Argentan debacle.

Much of Germany's army had been destroyed or captured in the final, awful battle at Falaise. What was left of German forces had fled across the Rhine, hoping for a miraculous last stand. Fortunately for Dorfmann, he was as far as possible from the front—while also being a safe distance from Berlin.

It wouldn't be long there before there were recriminations and state-mandated suicides. Dorfmann wasn't planning to fall on his sword, like that unfortunate Von Kluge. No, he would make every effort to avoid Berlin, and every excuse not to return if ordered there. Besides, with the Russians coming at them from the East, Dorfmann wanted to make sure he surrendered to the Allies if and when the time came.

Meanwhile, the war was far from over. But with the Allies pressing in from the west, and the Russians threatening the east, Nazi Germany was more like a caged, cornered wolf than a beast on the hunt.

No matter how much cognac he drank, Dorfmann never

would have expressed such sentiments to anyone. The Gestapo would have him strung up on a meat hook.

In point of fact, it was his job to instill hope on the home-front and inspire the troops in the field. Not an easy job these days.

He took another sip of cognac and smacked his lips.

What he needed was a good story for *Luftpost*. He needed a hero.

Dorfmann searched his mind.

He kept coming back to the young sniper, Dieter Rohde. He seemed to have been killed in the fighting at the Falaise Pocket. He had not much liked Rohde, who seemed impertinent and more interested in personal glory than Germany's. No matter. It would not take a great deal of fiction to cast him as a hero.

A dead hero was the best sort in that he couldn't turn out to be a disappointment later.

Unfortunately, Rohde's immediate commander, Hauptmann Fischer, had also been lost in the battle. There had been a real soldier.

In the sort of rousing prose meant to inspire the troops, Dorfmann described Rohde's heroic last stand, holding off Allied troops so that the last of the wounded could be carried to safety across the ford at Gue de Moissy. He inserted an entirely fictitious report that the American General Patton had demanded to know how one German sniper could stop the advance.

Satisfied, Dorfmann pulled the typewritten page from his typewriter, made a few corrections in pencil, and passed it along to his typesetter.

In several large boxes that he always carried with him, Dorfmann kept various props to be used in staged photographs. He went to a box now and rummaged about until he found what he was looking for, which was an Iron Cross.

The photo shoot cost him two bottles of his precious cognac. He was in a hurry, and he had found that the carrot worked so much better than the stick.

He secured a white cross that would be used to mark a grave, and had a clerk pound it into the yard out back. Dorfmann himself pushed the tacks into the wood, so that he could affix the Iron Cross to the grave marker. Technically, the Iron Cross was worn over the left blouse pocket of the uniform tunic—over the heart—but a couple of tacks would work for what Dorfmann had in mind. Then he assembled six soldiers to stand at attention to one side of the grave, marked by the cross. They made a passable honor guard. Dorfmann himself took the photographs and processed them. He already had a headshot of Rohde, which he would include. The young soldier had been a handsome devil.

He was pleased with the story and photographs; in a single afternoon he had concocted his lead story. After a moment's thought, he sent the article and copies of the photographs along to *Völkischer Beobachter*, the official publication of the Nazi party, distributed nationwide. The editors there would be glad to feature it prominently. It was likely that even The Leader himself would read the story.

Rohde had gotten his Iron Cross, after all. Dorfmann did not bother to submit the paperwork, which was not likely to make it through the increasingly chaotic channels, anyway. No matter. Rohde and his Iron Cross were going to be front-page news, which was as real as anything could be.

Dorfmann added a bit of cognac to his glass, and feeling pleasantly intoxicated now, raised the glass as if making a toast. "Prost," he muttered, then drank.

Germany had another dead hero.

Rohde would have been happy, *die kleine Scheisse.*

* * *

LIKE AN ISLAND IN A STORM, Lisette's farmstead had ridden out the battle mostly unscathed. She and the children returned three days after Cole had rushed them to safety. With other refugees from the fighting, she had taken shelter in a refugee camp behind the lines but close enough to hear the artillery.

She had prayed that there would be a home to return to.

Some of the old people seemed content to remain in American custody, but Lisette felt too much like a herded sheep. The Americans were trying to keep the refugees corralled almost like prisoners because they feared that members of the Wehrmacht—or worse yet, the SS—would try to escape by posing as refugees.

However, Lisette and the children did not attract much attention from the American MPs, so she had managed to slip away, starting out on foot with the children.

She had picked up a few more words of English in the last few days and managed to communicate to the driver of an American supply truck that she needed a ride.

At first, he had been reluctant.

"I don't know if it's a good idea, miss," the soldier said.

If she had not understood all of the words, she had understood his tone.

"Please," she said, putting a note of desperation in her voice.

The young soldier finally nodded. "If you really want to go, I'll take you."

She and the children had climbed into the back of the truck.

On the day that General Eisenhower was inspecting the ruins of nearby Argentan and viewing the Corridor of Death, Lisette returned to the farm.

Lisette had no desire to see where the heart of the fighting had taken place. There were enough corpses along the roadsides as it was, most of them German. The Allies had done what they could to quickly retrieve and bury their own dead in the summer heat. Eventually, the German dead would get burial in a mass grave.

The children seemed fascinated at first by the bodies, but then grew bored with the sight. They were more worried about how their old dog had fared.

Lisette did not have the heart to tell them that the dog had likely perished. How could he possibly have survived?

When the farm came into sight, Lisette slapped the tail-gate and the driver let her out.

The truck slowly pulled away, and Lisette inspected the damage. Pockmarks showed where a spray of bullets had struck the front of the farm cottage. There was a charred hole in the thatched roof of the barn. She could see the churned earth where shells had struck. Miraculously, the farm had survived the battle relatively unscathed.

With pounding heart, she walked around the corner into the farmyard, fully expecting to see Rohde's body and those of the other soldiers.

The bodies had disappeared, likely thanks to one of the burial crews. She gave thanks for that much.

Rohde. How could one ever forget what he had done to her or to Leo? She thought of him less now as her lover than as her defiler, a monster that she had harbored her bed. One could not forget something like that, she decided, but neither did one always have to remember. She decided to bury his memory in the darkest root cellar of her mind.

While she stood there taking it all in, their dog appeared from around the corner of the cottage. Leo and Sophie wrapped their arms around him gleefully.

"You must be starving, poor thing." She gave him some of

the crackers that she had gotten from the Americans. He wolfed them down. Some of her chickens had also survived, so at least they would have a few fresh eggs.

Over the next couple of days, Lisette worked to put things in order as best she could. The larger projects, like the hole in the barn roof, would have to await Henri's return.

To her surprise, he came limping into the farm a week later. He had been wounded in the leg and spent a few days in an Allied hospital, but the wound had not been severe. Many of the French Resistance fighters had volunteered to join the Allied forces taking the fight to Germany itself. With the Germans gone from their own countryside, Henri announced that he'd had enough of fighting. Henri put on his coveralls, and became a farmer once more, with Sophie and Leo tagging along beside him. Their old neighbors gave him something of a hero's welcome for fighting the Germans, and pitched in to help him make repairs.

It was a few days after that the American sniper, Cole, appeared.

"I just wanted to check up on you," he announced.

Henri's English was passable enough, and he translated. He seemed suspicious of the American at first, remembering the incident at the forward command post when Cole had pulled a knife on him, but instantly became more welcoming when Lisette explained that it had been Cole who took her and the children to safety just as the battle began. Henri greeted him warmly, and even gave the American a glass of red wine.

"You and your sister gettin' on all right?" Cole asked.

Henri grinned wryly and turned to Lisette. "He wants to know if I am still beating you."

Lisette reddened. The American was asking about Henri's reaction to the fact that Lisette had had a German soldier as a lover. Neither she nor Henri had made any mention of

Rohde since her brother's return. It was a subject that neither wished to discuss.

Henri straightened his shoulders and announced, "Lisette has done more for France than I have. She saved the farm and she saved my children. She is the true hero." He repeated the words in French for Lisette's benefit.

Cole finished his wine and stood. He had a graceful way of moving, an economy of motion, that made Lisette uneasy. He was no farmer. Cole looked so strange and out of place in their kitchen. The dull gleam of his rifle and the telescopic sight seemed somehow sinister. He smelled of sweat and gun oil. She realized that this man made her uncomfortable because he reminded her too much of her old lover, Rohde.

It was with a sense of relief that she watched him cross the farmyard and disappear into the fields. She tried to watch him out of sight, but an odd thing happened—the sniper Cole seemed to vanish into the landscape. One moment he had been there, and the next moment, he seemed to have disappeared.

Lisette shuddered and turned back into the kitchen. A stew bubbled on the stove. Henri sat with both children in his lap. For the first time, Lisette felt that for her, and for France itself, the war was finally over.

ABOUT THE AUTHOR

David Healey lives in Maryland where he worked as a journalist for more than twenty years. He is a member of the International Thriller Writers and a contributing editor to The Big Thrill magazine. Visit him online at:

www.davidhealeyauthor.com

or

www.facebook.com/david.healey.books